IT'S BARRY YOURGRAU AGAIN,
TAKING OFF THE TOPS OF OUR SKULLS AND LOOKING IN. . . .

THE SADNESS OF SEX

"Barry Yourgrau has a consistent, original voice. He is also a poet with a gift for compression . . . his tales are metaphors, rendered fresh by their imagery, their concrete and colloquial detail, odd and surprising denouements, and a real comic gift."

—*The New York Times Book Review*

"Yourgrau writes like a modern-day Morpheus with a rapier wit."

—*Entertainment Weekly*

"Vividly hallucinatory and often horrifyingly funny."

—*L.A. Style*

"Reading Barry Yourgrau is addictive, like putting peanuts in your nose and they turn into these spaceships or something."

—Roy Blount, Jr.

Please turn the page for more extraordinary acclaim . . .

"I can never remember my dreams, so Mr. Yourgrau's stories are a pretty good substitute."
—David Byrne

"Imagine Woody Allen reading a Raymond Carver story."
—*Oakland Tribune*

"These enchanting short takes . . . are odd, true, and thoroughly hilarious."
—Susan Cheever

"Yourgrau . . . suggests Woody Allen imitating Spalding Gray . . . a superb writer."
—*Los Angeles Times*

"What's wonderful about Barry Yourgrau's stories is that they have the uninhibited honesty of a dream being recounted by someone who's not yet wide awake."
—Susan Seidelman

"Yourgrau bravely bears witness to the wonderful lunacy of hope in the aftermath of idyllic love."
—Mark Richard, author of *Fishboy*

"Ineffably funny and sad."
—*San Francisco Examiner*

"Yourgrau provides surprises in the isolated corners of the mind, funny surprises—weirdly familiar surprises."

—*Los Angeles Times Book Review*

"Startling Rabelaisian grotesqueries and the primal imagery of Grimms' fairy tales."

—*Elle*

"His brief stories . . . evolve subtly into occasions for hilarity, dread, and pathos . . . his prose is precise as an English essayist's; he's drawn to the macabre underbelly of smiling domesticity."

—*L.A. Weekly*

"Barry Yourgrau manages to articulate your most bugged-out daydreams."

—Adam Horovitz (Ad Rock) of the Beastie Boys

"Wild but always literately delicious."

—*Variety*

THE SADNESS OF SEX

by

Barry Yourgrau

A Delta Book
Published by
Dell Publishing
a division of
Bantam Doubleday Dell Publishing Group, Inc.
1540 Broadway
New York, New York 10036

Library of Congress Cataloging in Publication Data
Yourgrau, Barry.
The sadness of sex / by Barry Yourgrau.
p. cm.
ISBN 0-385-31376-4
I. Title.
PS3575.094S23 1995
813′.54—dc20 94-20326
CIP

Designed by Alice Sorensen

Manufactured in the United States of America

Published simultaneously in Canada

March 1995

10 9 8 7 6 5 4 3 2 1

FFG

For my friends

Acknowledgments

I would like to express my special gratitude to Tom Schnabel, to Marti Blumenthal, to Matt Lewis Thorne and John Thorne, and Knight and Marcela Landesman. For their abiding aid and multiple generosities.

Heartfelt thanks as well to Aris Janigian, Bella Le Nestour and John Allen, Marci Miller, Lisa Jane Persky, Aaron Slavin, Toni Spencer and John Millei, and Garrett White.

Similarly, to Shelley Boris and Peter Lewis, Virginia Hatley, Wyatt Landesman, Peter Marren and Margaret Newman, and Robert Younger. And to my brother, Tug Yourgrau.

My appreciations to Henry Dunow and my editor, Steve Ross.

Support from the New York Foundation for the Arts and the Yaddo Corporation is gratefully acknowledged.

ACKNOWLEDGMENTS

Contents

1. The Horse 1
The Horse 3
Poison 6
Jumps 8
Lioness 10
Forsythia 11
Ferns 13
My Travels 15
Earth 17
Flora 19
Mermaids 22

2. Scenario 25
Scenario 27
Riddle 29
War 31
Sounds 33
Interlude 35
Du Lac 36
The Rampage 40
Tresses 42
Room Service 45
The Accident 47
The Waiting 49
Taboo 50
Bubble Gum 53

3. Domestic Intelligence 57
Domestic Intelligence 59
62 Earthquake
63 The Gun
66 Bay
68 Bucolic Days
69 Silver Arrows
73 The Raid and the Kiss
77 Horn
79 At the Neck
82 Operatives
84 Mysteries
87 Domestic Scene
89 Executrix
91 Ceasefire (Sentimental Culture)

93 Pigtails 4.
95 Pigtails
97 Beanie
99 Understanding
100 Androgyny
101 On Stage
103 My Business
105 Statue
107 Elephants
108 Acrobats
110 In Prison
112 Coins

115 Dark Hospital 5.
117 Dark Hospital

Contagion 119
Physiognomy 122
Lovers 127
Soliloquy 129
Moon 130
Ash 132
Burial 133
Palisades 134
Along the Boulevard 135
Fin de Siècle 137
Palmetto 140
Folk Painting 143

6. Snowfall 145
Snowfall 147
Pantry 149
Heart 151
In the Snows 153
Stone Fence 155
A Day's Work 157
Head 159
Corral 161

7. Tea 163
Tea 165
Elm 168
Glacier 175

181 Golden Age 8.
183 Golden Age
188 Island
190 The Sadness of Sex

201 Blossom 9.
203 Blossom
204 Apparition
206 Relics
209 The Visit
211 Night Thoughts
212 Toy
214 Poetry
216 Dust
221 In Memoriam
226 Interrogation
228 Above the Roofs
230 Practical Joke
232 The Fire

235 Blue 10.
237 Blue

251 At the Clockmaker's 11.
253 At the Clockmaker's

I could not help envying [him] . . . his troop of lithe, lissome, high-spirited, romping girls with their young supple limbs, their white round arms, white shoulders and brows, their rosy flushed cheeks, their dark and fair curls tangled, tossed and blown back by the wind, their bright wild saucy eyes, their red sweet full lips and white laughing teeth, their motions as quick, graceful and active as young antelopes or as fawns, and their clear sweet merry laughing voices, ringing through the woods.

—THE DIARY OF THE REV. FRANCIS KILVERT

My friend, the wisest among us should bless himself not to have met the woman, whether beautiful or ugly, intelligent or a fool, who could have driven him mad and sent him to the asylum.

—DENIS DIDEROT, "THIS IS NOT A STORY"

THE SADNESS OF SEX

1.
The Horse

The Horse

I BUY A HORSE FROM A WOMAN. ON THE WAY BACK TO MY PLACE, THE HORSE SUDDENLY FALTERS UNder me and collapses. I'm out in the middle of nowhere. The horse is finished. Its jaws are twisted open in a final grimace, its eyes glare up at nothing. I stare as its features begin incrementally to alter into those of a different beast. "Oh Christ," I think. "Not one of these!" I hurriedly pull free my saddle and as much of my bags as I can get clear, and drag them over to a boulder. I kneel behind cover, rifle in hand, a box of bullets beside me, watching as the horse continues its gruesome transformation. Scales have formed all over its body. Its tail swells out a long, coiled spike. Its muzzle broadens into a snout. Fangs protrude down over the bent bridle bit. Suddenly it twitches violently. It squeals, and then opens its gray jaws, and bellows. It slashes at the air with a clawed, reptilian hoof. It gives a mighty heave and struggles up onto its front knees. I start firing. The horse writhes and bellows, wildly flinging about the strands of the reins. Black blood sprays up. I reload frantically in a haze of gunsmoke, hearing the appalling roars and screeches. I look up to see the horse dragging itself toward me, its hideous tail uncoiling crazily, into the air, into the ground. I lunge over to the other side of the boulder and empty all my rounds from there. The horse sinks onto its haunches under the fusillade, squalling horribly, slowly and more slowly, pulsing jets of blood, one scaly leg thrust out at an impossible angle in front of it. Slowly it rocks over onto its side. I slump against the boulder with the emptied rifle. I pant, my limbs quaking. The ground about the horse is slick and marshy with dark blood. From high away through the silence come the first cries of the carrion birds.

A week later, when I'm fit for it, I go back to see the woman who sold me the horse. "Then it's finally happened to my stock," she murmurs. We're standing on her porch, in shadow, looking out at the corral. "I'm so very sorry," she declares quietly. "And you're sure you're alright?" She directs me a look that is part human concern, part business assessment. "I'm fine," I tell her. I shrug. "I've had it happen before. I knew what to do." "Well, I'll give you your money back," she says. "Come on inside. I won't offer you a replacement," she explains, "because they say once one's got it, the whole stock's that way." "That's what they say," I tell her. "But at least the stock will be safe for my use," she says, looking around to me with her hand on the screen door. "They say it only happens when the horse changes owners. Isn't that so?" I nod. "That's what they say," I agree.

She's a handsome woman. She runs the place by herself. When she invites me to stay for supper, I accept. "Unless of course you think the owner contracts the hazards of her animals," she says, with a cool, unembarrassed smile. "Isn't that what they say?" I grin quietly back. "That's not my thinking," I tell her.

Late that night, when I can't sleep, I get cautiously out of her bed and light a cigarette and lean against the planked wall by the window. I look out at the dark corral, under the dim, still-starry sky. The black shapes of the sleeping horses mingle with the bulks of the arid, primeval hills beyond. After a long while, I shift back around toward the interior of the room. I lean there by the window, gazing at the woman's sleeping head on the pillow, pondering all the forces in play.

Poison

I SIT IN A CAFÉ IN LATE MORNING. A GIRL HURRIES BY. SHE GIVES A DISTRACTED SMILE. SHE'S QUITE pretty. In an appealing way. I stare hurriedly down at my coffee. I stir it with a spoon that trembles. A while later, she goes by again. I can't stop myself: I look. She's not pretty, I realize. She's lovely! She's utterly, woundingly *lovely*! I groan and shift my shoes about on the floor and clutch the little round table with both hands. "Oh no," I think, tossing my head from one side to the other. "Oh no—no—*no*—" I wrench myself to my feet and plunge back out onto the sidewalk and lurch up against the side of the building, panting, chest heaving. Passersby turn their heads. I fumble over my face with a handkerchief, gasping and clenching my teeth. "You fool!" I upbraid myself. "You irresponsible fool!" I strike my thigh with my fist. I push off wildly and start tottering down the sidewalk. A pair of women on their way to late croissants shrink back out of my path ahead. Their outlines start to sway, slowly, ponderously, as if they were molten glass exposed to gusts of breeze. A terrible, icy shudder goes through me. The women squeal against a parked car as I give out a barking cry of protest and sink heavily to my knees a couple of yards before them. I twist about, this way and that, threshing the air with frantic, clamoring arms. "Help me! Help me!" I bleat, my cries lost in the women's rising screams. But it's too late. The hideous toxin of love has been ingested, and has taken. A spasm wracks my whole body, and powerfully and copiously, almost luxuriantly, down there on all fours, I begin to vomit out a tide of rose petals and perfume-bottle shards, and scraps of desperately scribbled, expensive notepaper. The whole adoring, noxious mess shoots and oozes over the pavement as the women shriek above me in horror, and writhe, and snatch up their feet to try to keep them clear.

JUMPS

I'M UP IN A SMALL PLANE. I'M IN THE BACK, WHICH IS DARK AND CROWDED WITH WOMEN. THE WOMEN WEAR party dresses. The air is thick with carousal, liquor splashes over everything, it spills onto dresses and bare arms and crooning throats, as the plane jostles in the air. I steal kisses fervidly. Finally a green light flashes on. Someone lurches over and pulls the door open. Light floods into the plane, and a fierce breeze throbs over us. One by one the women make their way to the doorway. They stand in it and scream in excitement, then they jump. For a moment they hover vertiginously over the whole earth, then their dresses are torn off, and the pretty tatters flurry above them and bloom out into huge, wind-swollen canopies. The women drift away through the sky, naked and swaying and moving their limbs this way and that, in attitudes of languid, overwhelmed pleasure. I can hear their wind-blown calls to me as I stand clutching desperately to the bulkhead by the door. Each woman who comes to take her turn presses warm kisses on me, pulls at me to join her. But inexplicably I resist, grinning white as a sheet. "I will, I will," I murmur, promising. But I can't, I'm paralyzed with fear. I stare out into the blaze of space, and my stomach dies away in me. I look down at the field of floating, naked bodies tossing on the bed of the air under their billowing, undulating sheets. I'm in a turmoil. I stagger back to the rear of the plane. There's a woman there. She blurts out that she's as terrified as I am. We laugh, a kind of hysteria of cowardly relief. We begin to paw furiously at each other, our eagerness, our frenzy, seething through us. The wind and light roar from the doorway. But try as we may, we can't seem to get our clothes off.

Lioness

I GO TO A MASQUERADE PARTY AND JOIN FORCES WITH A GIRL DRESSED UP AS A LIONESS. IN THE kitchen, squeezed in among the shouting throng by the refrigerator, we mutually construct a joke about my having a big chunk of raw meat in my pocket. "It's fresh and it's bloody," I shout. "From the choicest part of the carcass!" I exhibit an imaginary lump in my hand. "Now don't you take any of my fingers along with it," I cry warningly, grinning. The girl growls and waggles her tawny snout this way and that, so the big whiskers quiver. Suddenly she snaps at my hand with startling authenticity. I protest in surprise. "Savage! Savage!" I exclaim admiringly. She roars and lunges at me again, so I lurch back, and we burst out into raucous, overstimulated guffaws.

The party blares on and then grows late and turns seedy and nasty. The girl and I end up outdoors on the grounds somewhere, off among the bushes. Most of our festive apparel lies scattered about us. But she insists, swaying, on keeping her mask on. I sprawl back prone on my elbows, grimacing in a drunken haze as she crouches over my pale foot in the darkness. She begins to devour it. I gasp, and close my eyes. "I think I'm going . . . to regret this . . . in the morning. . . ." I hear myself observing, over the noise of her jaws.

Forsythia

It's women's washday. I pick my steps awkwardly along the cobblestones. At the top of the little road, a squat stone structure raises itself among the thorns and the forsythia bushes. It's the washhouse where the women go. Steam drifts up in voluptuous waves from the roof vents, toward the terraces of the gray clouds. I turn up the embankment, and get down and crawl along to my perch in the forsythia. I settle in with an idolator's practiced care. Furtively, I part the yellow bushes. There's a crack in the wall below. Through the mossy, dank stone I can spy into the heart of the steam. The women labor there companionably, their exposed flesh glowing pink and rude in the drifts of humidity. They have taken their privates out, and they scrub them with relish, kneading the pelts in the soapy water of the stone trough, lifting them out dripping and steaming, and slapping them vigorously against the trough's rim in glittering soapy sprays. Then they plunge them back into the steaming water.

Eventually the first ones emerge from the rear of the washhouse. They carry their spanking-clean prides over to the bushes and set them out to dry. Some of the pelts are wispy little swatches of gold, agleam and gossamer in the bland light. Others are great curly, hairy things, dark like kilt sporrans, like patches from goat hides. One in particular suggests a coarsely spun bird's nest. Its owner in fact resembles a large tousle-headed bird. The women are mindful of their modesty, now that they're out of doors. They loiter in their roughly gathered blouses and skirts and dresses. Their skin is ruddy from the washhouse as they chatter and laugh and share their cigarettes, and cast an eye up at the clouds, to see how the sun is making do. The sun strains in a golden blur, laboring to press its great round, hot face through for an unimpeded view taking.

From my screen of yellow forsythia, I take in this marvelous spectacle. These are heady days for me, magical ones, days to savor for a lifetime. My heart clangs like a church bell inside me, and my quickened breathing resounds in my ears over the amiable conversings of the women below me, and my elbows tremble under my weight. A dusty robin chirps nearby, and then swoops with a bustle of wings down onto the laden bushes, before a pink-armed hand waves it away.

Ferns

I EAT A SPECTACULAR LUNCH AND FALL ASLEEP ON THE WAY BACK HOME. I SPRAWL ON MY BACK IN A nest of ferns by the verdant path. The delicate fronds tremble to my snores. As I am in this state, a pair of hard-bitten female travelers come upon me. They stare at me over the ferns. They creep right up beside me, and peer down at my effectively comatose form. Slowly they exchange a deepening look of amusement and opportunity and unscrupulous conspiracy.

With slender, grimy fingers, nimble and made for the subtleties of tending infants, they set to work loosening my wallet from its hip pocket. The wallet is nut brown and heavy, swollen with the load of money that was the cause for my ill-advised midday celebration. At last they count the worn bills, trembling with astonished delight, their eyes widening above their sun-weathered cheeks. They embrace in sheer glee, with a whooping kiss so loud it resounds into the trees. In alarm they twist around together and stare at me. I shift about in my sleep among the ferns, my brow furrowed at the imaginary difficulties conjured up by my cloudy, sleeping brain to account for the sudden clamor. The women hold their breath and watch as I paw once at my nose and murmur an indistinct phrase, as old as the first beginnings of life, and then settle in more deeply, munching on nothing. My face resumes its expression of mild, trusting plenitude.

Around me the forest stands quiet. Late afternoon

spreads its still light and its ponderous shadows. The tiny fingers of the ferns tremble to my breathing as I sleep on, alone once more. Every once in a while a little string of belches manipulates my lips, as do remembrant mastications. I begin to snore. The slack, emptied wallet lies in the ferns beside me, where it was discarded.

My Travels

I COME DOWN WITH A BAD ATTACK OF STOMACH AILMENT, WHILE TRAVELING. I PAY SOME LOCAL WOMEN to care for me. They take the money I give them, then rob me of my valuables and beat me as I plead with them groggily from my couch. I lie bruised and unattended for almost two days in my rented bungalow. At last, covered with my own filth, I manage to crawl to the front door. My weak cries are heard by a passerby, who summons the police.

A doctor appears with medication, and arrangements are made to transfer me to the relative comfort of a hotel. A police official elaborately notes my description of my assailants in a baroque notebook, until the doctor insists on my need for rest and quiet. An old, malodorous ambulance arrives and rattles me off to the hotel, where a great wooden fan is waiting for me, majestically disturbing the air over my bed.

Within a week the police arrest a pair of suspects. I identify them positively. The local version of a trial commences. As befits my exotic life, I fall desperately in love with one of the defendants. She has a downy, passionate line of mustache on her lip, and her dark eyes flash brilliantly when she lies. I decide in the grip of my amours to withdraw all charges against her, and request an urgent conference with police and prosecutor. A stormy interview follows. The charges remain intact. I watch in wretchedness as my beloved is dragged off bellowing melodramatically through the door, to the years of horrendous servitude and isolation ahead of her. The police official turns in his seat, and fixes me with his implacable, brutal gaze. I blink off down at the floor.

With much emotion, I pack my bags that night. I leave at first light. I resume my travels once more, burdened as always with memories of illness, with my heart's newest tumult, with its ever-abiding anguish and regrets.

EARTH

THERE'S A CAVE-IN. TWO WOMEN ARE TRAPPED INSIDE THE EARTH. THE RESCUE PARTY STARTS DIGging with huge pneumatic machines. The rescuers' helmet lamps glow as they shout and crane forward, peering. A great floodlight glares in the chill darkness.

I sneak away with a shovel and a lamp. I know an alternative, quicker route to where the women are trapped. Behind a fallen tree trunk, icy and slimy with rot, I start digging. An hour later I disappear below the surface of the earth. I stop, panting, and stare up at the rim of the pit, above which the faint glow of the rescuers' lights tinges the dark night sky. Sweat runs down my neck. I can hear in the distance the pounding of the machinery. I clear my face and grip the shovel again and feverishly resume.

After another hour, I reach the streak of clay that tells me I'm almost to them. I throw the shovel aside and start clawing bare-handed at the pungent, caked earth. I fling the yellow clods behind me. Suddenly my arm plunges through. I tear out a hole and peer in. Stockings hang down in front of my eyes. There is light from a spirit lamp. The women recline on mats. They wear lounging pajamas. One of them rattles her glass at me. "Did you bring any ice?" she drawls lazily. Feverishly I start squirming in toward them through the dense, silky walls of the clay. The air ahead of me is warm and close, voluptuously scented. The women watch me, drowsily amused. I struggle, intoxicated, stabbed with despair at how short a time I will have with them. Already I can feel the earth trembling as I flap and wriggle, and the machinery pounds and gouges and approaches.

FLORA

EVERY TIME I KISS MY GIRLFRIEND, A FLOWER SPROUTS FROM THAT PLACE ON HER SKIN. AT FIRST this floral effulgence is delightful and winsome. But after a couple of months of it, the experience begins to pall.

I lie gloomily in our domestic bed, unable to suppress a curse after a peony has blossomed in my face in the midst of a nuzzle. "I'm sorry—" my girlfriend exclaims, as with deft practice she snaps off the splendid, pink-leafed bloom. We're both naked. "Yeah, yeah, yeah," I mutter ungraciously, removing the bits and scraps of petal from my lips. My girlfriend looks around sharply, her breasts jostling, from fitting in the peony beside a buttercup in a water glass. "Well, you don't have to act as if I'm doing it intentionally," she protests. I don't reply. I strive to maintain a grim equilibrium. I know it really isn't legitimate for me to make an issue of things, but all at once I can't stop myself.

"It's just, it would be so great—just once," I announce, "to be able to make love without feeling as if I had to hack my way into a florist's shop!" I indicate with a bitter wave the rows of vases and glasses, all bulging with floral cornucopia—a testimony to the lavishness of our attempted affections.

"Well you're not being fair at all!" she retorts fiercely. "I'm the one who has to take that horrid, useless medicine every night!" She waves in turn at the large brown bottle of flavored pesticide, and the big

Delft-handled tablespoon beside it with which she serves her dose at bedtime. I grunt and turn away, glowering, rubbing an exasperated hand into the side of my head. After several thick, grim moments, I become aware of a whimper and sniffing. Anger lashes up through me. Venomously I swing around. Her own head hangs, she clutches a hand herself to her brow, while she trembles and sobs. "It's just . . . not . . . fair," she sputters softly. For an instant my anger wallows huge, then suddenly I take in her forlorn nakedness, her girlish, concave shoulders with their magnificent burden of her lovely head, and all around us the preposterous bounty of flowers.

"I'm sorry," I blurt out. "I'm so sorry, darling—come here!" I bring her to me and fold her up in my arms. "There, there, you sweetest thing," I console, and I close my eyes, and the old tenderness floods us. But then a mass begins to prod my nose. I maneuver around it. Finally we have to separate, while, to her murmured apologies and groans of frustration, she breaks the several flowers off one by one. She flings them out onto the carpet. Then it's just too much for her, and she sinks onto the pillows away from me, weeping to herself, bitterly, hopeless. I lie pressed against her from behind, keeping close but being careful with my lips. "It's okay, it's okay," I try to assure her. "It'll be alright." With glum eyes I stare off beyond the arc of her moist, trembling cheek. A delayed-blooming poinsettia pops out above her eyebrow, like a floppy, scarlet star.

Later, when she's fallen asleep, I ease out of bed. I pull on some clothes and let myself softly out. I follow my feet as they lead me ambling along in the company of my thoughts. I make my way, shaking my head at things, sighing over my connubial quandary. It's deep, languid summer, and despite the very late hour, couples are still about, luxuriating in the warmth and the shadows. I drift to an envious halt, and stand gazing along my shoulder at a pair kissing fondly, propped against a tree. Their doting mouths plant bleary, tender kisses everywhere, without obstruction.

Mermaids

I GO TO SEA. FOR VARIOUS REASONS, I FALL OVERBOARD. I STRUGGLE IN THE WAVES FOR A FEW MINutes, and then the mermaids close around and drag me down struggling with them, and in due course I breathe only water, and I drown. I drift and bump down among the gamboling horde, into their gray-green, hazy world. They laugh, and push me and pet me, in ignorance of my condition, my sad, human flaw. When they see finally how weary and lifeless and agog I've become, they prop me against a glossy boulder on the sea floor, and they crown my slumped head with a wreath of sea flora, and drape my neck with long dark sashes of weed. In my lolling hand they set a round, bladdered creature that swells and puffs and turns all shapes in its consternation. They make merry crowning me the idle king of their festivities: a white, pulpy bosom pushes into my nose as one of the company slowly tumbles across me, and then twists herself back around, and laughing, trails the gossamer frills of her great tail across my open, unbreathing mouth, to the amusement of her sisters.

So they treat me, there far below on the sea floor. The days pass one after another, and time loosens and drifts with the great workings of the water. My drowned flesh softens; slowly rots; dissolves into muck. The mermaids are fond of me, and they clean my bones for me. They decorate my frailty, waving the long, slimy grass of their black hair over my flimsy ribs. Into the barren, staring sockets of my eyes they set lumps of colored stone, little porous fool's treasures from the mouths of caves. They freshen my weedy raiments, and kiss my bony brow, and maintain me in state as the stiff, spindly mascot suzerain of their revels, of their empire many fathoms below, in the secret places of the waves. . . .

2.

Scenario

Scenario

"WHO *ARE* THOSE PEOPLE?" I ASK THE GIRL. "I DON'T KNOW," SHE MUTTERS. SHE LOOKS PERTURBED AND introspective. "Just keep rowing," she insists. I strain at the oars. One of them lurches up wildly out of the oar-lock. I curse and fumble to get it back in place. The boat veers about. "What are you doing!" the girl demands. "What the hell do you think I'm doing?" I protest, wrenching this way and that. "I'm not a boatman!" At last I manage to propel us into the cover of a shady bank, under an overhanging bough.

Through the leaves we watch the figures stealthily probing out from the opposing greenery into the sunlight. They scan the pond. They all wear dark, formal suits and the somberly festive asterisks of carnations. "Who can they be?" I mutter. The girl doesn't answer. She sits leaning forward intently, her eyes hard and watchful. I look at the bright blue ribbon in her curly hair, at the powder pink hue of her waitress uniform. Suddenly these take on the aspects of masks, of almost sinister, adopted guises. I move my eyes down to the small, odd-looking leather handbag tucked carefully against her on the seat. "Is there something hazardous and extremely valuable in your bag?" I whisper, with an inspired flare of insight. She doesn't respond. Across the way the figures move slowly along in and out of the trees. "Don't you dare touch it," the girl murmurs at last, without shifting her gaze, her voice cold and dangerous, as the afternoon sunlight plays over the pond.

RIDDLE

I WAKE UP. IN BED NEXT TO ME IS A WOMAN I HAVE NEVER SEEN BEFORE. I STARE AT THE SLEEPING face. I have no idea who she is. I look around the dim room. Its heavy curtains are drawn. There is a bureau and mirror, an armchair with a hodgepodge of clothing on it, more clothes scattered on the frayed oriental rug on the floor. I have never seen any of these things before.

I lift the covers away gingerly and put my bare feet on the floor. Again I look down at the sleeping face. I shake my head. I look around the room once again, running my hand through my hair. I rise and pad over to the curtains and peer through. The street scene is completely unfamiliar. I turn back to the room, slowly. I try to remember what happened last night. I can't seem to. My heart gives a sudden, sickened jolt: I realize that I can't in fact remember anything whatsoever. I try to think of my own name. I gape about wildly. There are trousers on the armchair. I rush over. In a back pocket is a wallet. It contains some dollar bills. Otherwise it's empty. I begin frantically digging through the other pockets of the trousers. The sound of a voice makes me gasp.

"Who are you?"

The woman is lying pressed back against the headboard with the covers drawn up around her chin, as if protecting herself. The look on her face is a mixture of alarm and confusion, as if she weren't sure she had woken or were still dreaming.

I try to smile at her, in reassurance, torturedly. I open my mouth, but then I just begin shaking my head. I raise a hand and make a gesture indicating my helplessness at answering her simple, eternal question. "I don't know," I confess, almost tearfully, hearing how sickly and absurd my voice sounds. I stare at the woman dismally in the gloom. "Who are *you*?" I ask.

A long, peculiar silence follows this. The woman's eyes seem to widen in the increments of a slowly deepening, bewildered horror. They shift about the room, from one side to the other, before resettling on me. At last the woman speaks, in a small, stricken voice. "I don't know," she says.

WAR

I GO FOR A WALK ALONG A BEACH. THE LATE AFTERNOON GROWS FOGGY AND DARK. I LOSE TRACK OF where exactly I am. I hear someone nearby. "Who is it?" a voice demands sharply. "Don't be alarmed," I call back. "I'm just out for a—" There's a gun blast, and I keel over backward onto the wet sand.

I wake up in a makeshift hospital. The attendant explains to me that there's a war going on. "But I never heard anything about it before," I reply, in groggy consternation from my wound. "It's been going on a long time," the attendant says. "I don't know, it seems like forever." At various times the noise of distant gunfire comes to my ears. The attendant wears guerrilla-style khakis and carries a weapon. He's both guard and nurse, I'm not sure exactly of the distinction. At first, in the haze of my injury, I take him for a kid. Then at a certain point, I realize in fact he's not a guy at all, he's a girl.

I watch her stand peering out the barred little window, her cigarette flicked aside, her eyes screwed up in concentration at what she surveys. This is after a particularly close-sounding burst of gunfire. I hear her grunting to herself. "What's going on?" I call out feebly. There's a long pause. I start to ask again. "Nothing," she mutters. She makes a vague silencing gesture toward me. After a while, she turns and comes thoughtfully over to my bed. She leans her weapon against a chair and begins to check my bandages. "Will you be keeping me here long?" I ask her. I shift about to accommodate her handling. "I was just out for a walk, you know. I really didn't do anything," I point out. "I'm an innocent." The attendant tugs the bandages with rough care as she pins them anew. "It's not up to me," she says. "It all depends on what my orders are." She gives my shoulder a little pat and fashions the hint of a brusque smile. "Your wound is healing pretty good," she says. She looks down at me, and clears the hair from my brow.

I spend a lot of my time in bed dozing away the long hours in the half-companionable ache of my wound. I fall right to sleep, sometimes, in the afternoon. Once, when I open my eyes after such an occasion, the attendant is performing a crude, modest toilette at a basin on the corner table. I watch her in silence from my pillow. Her camouflage shirt is partially undone, and she reaches in with a sponge and slowly wipes herself and squeezes the sponge out quietly into the basin. I glimpse a portion of intimate flesh. I gaze at its fleeting, transfixing image, at the beautiful sturdiness of her throat. The sound of gunfire breaks into the tableau. The attendant stiffens. She lowers the sponge. She lunges out to the side and snatches up her weapon, and leans with her shoulder pressed against the wall, in her opened shirt, staring out the window.

Sounds

I LIE WITH A GIRL IN BED. SUDDENLY I RISE ON AN ELBOW. I LOOK AT HER. "WHAT'S THAT?" I ASK. "What is what?" she says. "That noise, outside," I tell her. I prop myself up on my hand. "You don't hear it?" I ask. She raises herself also. She listens. "I don't hear anything," she says. "Are you serious?" I tell her. "You can't hear some kind of animal suffering out there? A dog or something? You can't hear it whimpering?" The girl frowns into the lamplight, concentrating. She's young. Her face has the mildness of a child's. She shakes her head. "Maybe it's one of those sounds only guys hear," she suggests, with the flicker of a grin. I snort and make a disapproving gesture. "I'm going to go out and see what it is," I declare. I pull on trousers over my pajamas and get barefoot into my shoes. I find a flashlight in the drawer by the bed. "Maybe a racoon got hold of a dog," I speculate, scowling. I give a shiver. "Jesus, what a dismal hue and cry," I mutter. "If this keeps up all weekend . . ." The girl blinks sleepily, on her face a look of concern but no real comprehension.

I let myself out through the screen door onto the back steps. The sounds are coming from around the side of the bungalow. They're long quaverings of intimate, wounded protest. I edge along, the beam of light leading my way and warning of my oncoming presence. The stars glint above in the enormous, black, grand sky. I reach the corner of the bungalow and with a catch of breath I throw the light around over the siding and out onto the rough lawn and the pines. Nothing shows. The weak, incessant cries beseech the night stillness. I take a couple of uncertain steps forward, sweeping the darkness with the light beam. But the grass is empty, and the trees stand solemn and unoccupied. I remain there for several minutes, profoundly perplexed, with the suffering protests rising from close by. "What in hell's name . . ." I mutter, banging at my thigh with the heel of my fist. Finally, at a complete loss, I turn around.

When I come back into the bedroom, the girl is sitting quietly on the side of the bed. She looks up at me. "Now I hear something," she declares. She inclines her head, to attend. "Can you hear that?" she murmurs. "Isn't it beautiful? It's some kind of songbird. Maybe a nightingale. Do they have actual nightingales around here?" she wonders. I listen beside her, scowling. All I can hear are the same inexplicable complaints of animal distress. I stir a slack hand, grimacing in frustration, almost despair. The girl looks off with her head uplifted, her eyes half-closed, an expression of gentle transport on her smiling, youthful face.

INTERLUDE

"WHAT'S HAPPENING?" SAYS THE GIRL. SHE SITS ON THE EDGE OF THE BED AND STARES OUT WITH AN open mouth through the dark window at the roofs of the town. Flames sluggishly engulf the tops of the houses, leaping slowly and then surging, swaying. "It's nothing. Another fire," I mutter in a disinterested voice. I reach out a hand and pull her down quietly by her bare, brown arm. I loll over her, nuzzling her shoulder, her neck. Her flesh has a musky, healthy odor, like that of a clean animal, wild but benign. I murmur this in her ear and she gives a low laugh and soon after grows passionate.

Later we lie in silence. With an elbow propped in the pillows, she stares out somberly at the vista of the flames. I lie behind her, gazing at my finger as it slowly traces the swelling prominence of her brown, bare flank. The light from the fire plays over it, flickering and faintly gilding.

Du Lac

I CRAWL THROUGH A WINDOW. IN THE DARKNESS OF A ROOM I SET FIRE TO THE BED. I RETREAT TO THE WINdow, watching the flames heave and surge as I urinate into the drapes. When the fire erupts onto the ceiling I fumble with my trouser buttons and clamber back over the sill and make off along the sloping tiles of the hotel roof.

The next morning each of the guests is asked to appear in the hotel manager's office. "Last *night* . . ." I repeat, when my turn comes. "Well, let's see . . . I had dinner in the dining room. Afterward I came out onto the terrace for a drink. . . .

"And then I felt like taking a walk," I recall. "I went down to the lake. I strolled along for a while, admiring the moonlight on the water. Then I looked the other way, and my eyes fell on the flowers beside the path. How pretty they looked, all asleep and tucked in for the night in their beds! I stopped. Something came over me. I've never done this before—I couldn't control myself, I bent down—I picked a flower! And then another! And then another and another and another! Yes, there were signs forbidding such a practice—signs everywhere!

"I resumed my walk, illicit prize clutched in hand. With every step my sense of guilt grew stronger. What had I done? What had I done! Suddenly I couldn't bear it, I turned and flung the sinful bouquet into the lake and hurried away. But instead of relieving the weight of my transgression, this impulsive act seemed only to intensify the burden! With a cry of anguish I stopped in my tracks and heaved about and went rushing back to the spot (by the wrought-iron bench) where I had thrown the flowers in. Vainly I searched the dim lapping surface for a blossom. Nothing! In a panic I leapt from the path and plunged fully clothed into the dark waters. The murky, roiling depths yielded still no sign. Flailing and choking I struggled up for air, and dove once more, determined to recover the flowers—

"And that's when I saw . . . *something*! . . . Something that froze the very blood in my veins! . . .

"A monstrous snake—a great sea serpent—was coiling and uncoiling toward me, through the lugubrious deep! . . . Mesmeric its cold skin shimmered, all gliding opal and brushed silver and steel! . . . In a moment it was upon me, it had wound its great cold self around me. Its terrible head came writhing slowly up to mine—and I saw my end, I tell you, I saw my own numbed death rising to meet me! But what greeted my eyes wasn't a serpent's hideous snout at all—no! No!—it was the face—of a lascivious young girl! She smiled at me—lewdly!—and then—she kissed me!!

"How many minutes, how many hours did she hold me down there, twisting and helpless in her chill embrace, while she ravaged my mouth with her kisses—kisses half-foul with the mud and weeds of the lake bottom? . . . How many hours, how many lugubrious ecstasies torn unceasing from my lips? . . . At dawn I discovered myself crumpled up on the path against the foot of the bench, somehow miraculously unscathed but for a sore neck, my clothes miraculously dry and intact. And there, beside me on gravel, lay the flowers! In a daze I gathered them up. I'm ashamed to admit what I did then—I went right over to the nearest flowerbed and stuffed the blossoms back in among their fellows, in the clumsy hope they'd pass undetected. Then I staggered back up to my room, exhausted, and fell into a deep, dreamless sleep. . . ."

I clear my throat. There's silence. I shift in my chair. "Anyway, that's where I was last night," I mumble. "You asked me, and that's what I did. . . ."

There's another silence. The hotel manager stares at me. Slowly, thoughtfully, the immaculate, bald dome of his head begins to nod. "Yes . . ." he says. "Well. That's certainly a satisfactory account of your actions. As far as we're concerned." He clears his throat. *"Très profond . . ."* he adds. He stares at me. One of his eyelids twitches. He smiles. The lid twitches again. He gets to his feet. "Now don't you worry about the flowers," he says. He comes around his desk. "What's a few tulips, more or less?" He laughs expansively. He extends a hand. I shake it. He holds on. "I'm sure you understand," he says intensely, "if we ask for the time being that you refrain absolutely from recounting these experiences of yours to anyone, anywhere, beyond the walls of this room. . . ."

In the afternoon there is a commotion outside my door. I open it a crack. Two harried policemen are trying to hustle a fat, middle-aged woman down the corridor. The big dame wriggles and curses, brandishing her handcuffed wrists and bellowing about false arrest. An audience of faces peers at the scene from doorways down both long sides of the passage. The cops look discomfited and extremely irked. One of them gets an elbow in the nose. I close my door silently and turn the latch, my mind full of thoughts.

Sometime after midnight I make my way along the hotel roof. I pause in the cover of a chimney, to adjust the sack of matches under my jacket. I gaze back down over my shoulder at the black expanse of the lake. In the distance I can make out the silhouette of the wrought-iron bench, and a bald-headed figure beside it. One hand appears to be clutching the bench, the other is stretched out as if to implore the lapping waters. I leave the chimney's shadow and start across the moon-lit tiles. Ever so faintly, bits and pieces of awkward, passionate obscenities drift up to me from the edge of the lake.

The Rampage

Down in the village, a woman has run amok. The thresholds of the cottages are slippery with blood. An old man lies face down by a rosebush, the flies probing at his neck where the ax blade struck him. A child wails in the hot afternoon.

Eventually the madwoman is cornered in a shed used to store grain. The villagers are backward country folk, and they stand around mild mannered and stunned, not knowing what to do with their quarry now that they've got her trapped. One of them edges fearfully into the doorway, then with a scream of fright comes dashing out.

I take in the scene from the rear of the crowd, having wandered over from some shade. I turn away, rubbing my jaw. I grunt to myself. I go over to a stand of bushes and start picking a handful of wildflowers. I push my way back through the crowd to the door. The village folk make way for me, murmuring. I square my shoulders and very carefully press the door in wider, and extend the flowers ahead of me.

The woman is crouched in the middle of the dirt floor, ax on high in the dimness. Her arms and lank, wild hair are spattered with blood. She snorts like a bull at the sight of me. But the flowers confound her. A dopey look spreads over her face. "Here, for you," I address her in a quiet, intimate voice, smiling, offering the bouquet toward her with a gesture of friendliness and calm. "Lovely flowers. All for you." She stares at them. Her head sinks forward and she stares at me. "Yes, all for you," I insist. Gingerly I back the door almost closed behind me. "Pretty flowers, for a pretty lady," I murmur. I slide a step forward. "Take them," I urge, smiling. "They're all yours. . . . Take them. . . ." There's a long, ponderous silence, a primal watching in the dim, close air. I inch another step.

She rocks against a sack of grain, clutching the violet and yellow blooms to her bosom with one hand. She stares at the earthen floor. Tears run down her heavy, disordered face. I kneel on my haunches in the spill of kernels and seeds, leaning close, whispering tender nothings, stroking with a delicate hand the sticky flesh of her bare, heavy arm. I hear her low groans and gulped breathing as I sweet-talk her. My eye is fixed on the awful thing still resting in her grip against her thigh. Eventually, cooing and softly protesting my tenderest affections, I'm able to work my hand down uncontested. I lift the ax away, and remove its horror to the dirt behind me. Flies buzz over us in the shadowy stillness. The door creaks open behind me, and breathless faces fearfully peer in.

Tresses

I'M WALKING DOWN THE STREET. A WIND COMES UP. I CLUTCH MY HAND TO MY HEAD, OUT OF FEAR OF MY hair blowing off. Then with a snort, I take my hand away. "What can I be thinking of?" I wonder. "I don't wear a wig, my hair'll be fine." The wind freshens. Two women come toward me, hurrying along the other side of the street. A gust rushes over them, making an uproar with their skirts. They beat at the surging hems, trying to secure them with stiffened arms as they clatter along in their hasty progress. I stop and regard them. "How truly bizarre," I exclaim to myself. "They're both quite bald!" I watch as they head over pointing to a certain tree and begin straining on tiptoe to reach into the branches. They flounder with outstretched hands.

One of them glances around suddenly. The sunlight gleams on the bony globe above her ears. She spies me and hurriedly whispers to her companion. The two of them watch over their shoulders in consternation as I step across the street toward them. "Pardon, ladies, but I couldn't help noticing your efforts," I exclaim simply, as I reach their curb. "Perhaps I could be of some assistance?" I suggest. They look at me with blank, reddened faces. They glance at each other. There is a palpable air of embarrassment about them, of exposure, even shame. Their pale, unadorned skulls appear almost luridly intimate and naked. I find myself blushing at their silence. I peer up into the tree. "Aha!" I announce, on a note of comprehension. "I see them up there!"

Among the branches are visible the results of wind-blown havoc: two robust heads of hair, one auburn, one black. They're like domestic creatures that have bolted away. The wind gusts violently. The women cry out and make motions of hapless alarm. "Don't worry, I'll get them for you," I declare. I leap from the ground and stab both hands into the thrashing leaves. I come down with the auburn hair. It's big and silky and almost alive in my fingers. One of the women grabs it from me. "What about mine?" protests the other. "I'll get it, not to worry," I assure her. I leap again. I can't reach the target. There's another gust. The woman gives a stricken cry. "It's going to blow away—" she wails. "Stop it! Stop it!" Hectically I rejump. The leaves flounder in my face. I come down heavily, empty-handed. The woman covers her mouth in anguish. Her companion looks on with her fingers clamped into her auburn tresses, securing them fast. Again the wind surges. The bald woman screams. Her skirt storms. I curse and step back and then stalk forward and launch myself upward. I flail through the greenery that pokes at my face and descend wildly and lurch several steps to get my balance. I have various parts of a number of branches, and the hair. The woman lunges over and seizes it from me. Hurriedly she crams the coarse jet mass down over her bare poll. "Thank you, oh thank you," she murmurs. "You're very—welcome," I pant. Dazedly I pluck and brush at the leaves and twigs over my clothing. The two women regard me, standing side by side in their coifs. *"Thank you!"* they call out in unison. I lift my hand in self-deprecation. An awkward, windblown pause ensues. The women glance at each other. Without further ado, just like that, they turn to go. "Thank you *so much,*" the auburn one adds back over her shoulder, with intent earnestness, as they hurry off.

I stand bemused in the litter of branch bits, chest still heaving, watching them disappear down the side-walk. They keep one hand fastened to the tops of their prodigal locks and the other guardingly into their skirts. I give a wan, half-ironic gesture of valediction after them. The wind swarms around my knees, stirring up the scent of torn leaves. I feel my hair suddenly fly straight up, in cartoon fashion, until scowling I furiously clap a hand on it.

Room Service

I WORK IN A HOTEL. I TAKE FOOD UP TO THE GUESTS IN THEIR ROOMS: BREAKFAST, LUNCH, DINNER, snacks, drinks. Late ice. I keep hoping for adventures, but nothing seems to happen. One night an old, obviously dying gent wheezes his order over the phone in a gasping whisper. He hints at a shocking, possibly lucrative confession if I hurry. I arrive sweating outside his room with his tray. The door is ajar. A group of figures are crowded inside. "Did he die?" I blurt uncouthly, coming into the lamplight with the order. "Did who die?" someone asks. "The old guy," I tell him. "What old guy?" says someone else. "The room's empty. That stupid marmot from next door escaped into here somehow." "Will you close the damn door!" someone shouts at me.

Another night a pair of sisters get me up into their suite and won't let me out. I decide to make the most of it, even though it could cost me my job. I come out of the bathroom in just my shoes and socks and boxer shorts. I strike a bawdy pose. But there's no response. They've passed out together on the sofa. I go over glumly beside them and finish off the champagne, swigging from the bottle. I stare at the remains of their supper on the cozily lit table, at the sick-spilled clothes flung on the carpet. Out in the distance, beyond their snores, the boats sound in the famous harbor. The moonlight falls gauzy and atmospheric through the lazing curtains of the French windows. I sit for a long while with the empty bottle. Finally I shrug and get dressed and let myself out. The next day I watch the sisters off. They wear conspicuous sunglasses and display not the slightest recognition of me.

I ask one of the other, older, waiters confidentially what he thinks of all this. He lifts his shoulders, philosophical. Room service is a trade, like any other, he says. Adventure and romance are always somewhere else, always what the other guy is up to. He trails off, and strokes his nostrils with long, bony fingers. My bemusement at his words emboldens me. I ask him straight out, perplexed, about the history of the tiny, gleaming, gold heart set into the actual flesh of one of his knuckles. He glances at it scornfully. "Ah, nothing worth talking about," he replies. He pulls a face and makes a gesture. "Some lady guest," he mutters. "But surely—" I protest, but then the order phone rings. And in a moment he flips his towel over his arm and blandly winks at me and trudges out the door.

THE ACCIDENT

A CARRIAGE HAS TURNED OVER IN THE ROAD. THE COACHMAN IS SPRAWLED MOTIONLESS NEAR IT. The horses mill about in a neighboring field, trembling and snorting. The broken traces hang loose among them, like elaborate, old-fashioned sickroom devices. A woman lies pinned beneath the carriage. Her head and shoulders protrude into the dust of the road. Her hat and veil are crumpled askew. What is visible of her clothing is plush and gray and expensive looking. She moans, barely conscious. I stand at the road's edge, gazing down at her beauty, at the poetic image of her loveliness fixed in the catastrophic setting. A wooden carriage wheel continues to spin and clang in the silence. Then hooves and cries sound behind me, and the rush of ministrations shoves me aside. I wander off down the road, pausing every now and then to regard the scene. A group of men struggle with the mass of the carriage, raising it with straining slowness off the ground.

I put up for the night at a local inn. I sit at a table in a corner, gazing off with my thoughts. The accident victim has been brought here for the night before going on to the hospital in the main town some distance off. The local doctor has been summoned, has appeared, is sequestered in the bedroom at the top of the stairs. I wander over and inquire of the barmaid what she knows of the accident, and of the victim's identity. The barmaid snorts. The coachman was probably drunk, she tells me. The horses bolted, the carriage ran over a stone, twisted a wheel, the traces broke and the whole business was thrown over. The injured party is apparently very wealthy. And very pretty, too, the barmaid adds, shoving my refilled glass in front of me. I lift my head. I look at her, my eyebrows raised at the tone in her voice. "Are her injuries grave?" I ask coolly. The barmaid regards me likewise. "Nothing money and beauty won't easily mend," she observes, with a salty, hard-knocked grin.

Sometime well after midnight, the barmaid finally joins me in the barn. She displays the bottle of liquor she's come away with. We share it on the straw. The moon seems to wobble in the unpaned window. The barmaid laughs at the things I say, and slaps at my fumblings and liberties. One of us finally has the inspiration of bringing the wheelbarrow over. Half-unlaced, the barmaid wriggles down on her back, and I turn the barrow over on her, and heated and gasping and laughing with delight at ourselves, we prepare to take our pleasure. From the straw, she sends up peals of laughter at me as I kneel over her, bemused and stirred to silence once more by the evocation of what transpired in the road.

The Waiting

The plaza is deserted under the moon. In the colonnade of one facade stand a row of women. They are bare to the waist. They look off in all directions: silent, impassive. Perhaps they are waiting for someone.

A long shadow moves on the flagging at the far end of the colonnade. It moves in and out of the columns. It is a young boy, like me. He is looking for the red ball one of the giant women holds at her naked waist.

Taboo

I'M ROMANTICALLY INVOLVED WITH A CANNIBAL. MY FRIENDS DISAPPROVE. "LISTEN," THEY BEGIN UNcomfortably, "far be it from us to interfere in matters of the heart. But really, how can you—" But I interrupt them. "I won't hear a word against her," I inform them. "She's a marvelous, one-of-a-kind girl, and I adore every inch of her, from right this minute until beyond forever." "Yes, well and good," they reply, shifting about in their seats. "Wonderful! But surely you realize, ultimately, this relationship just is not healthy. More than that—it's positively *dangerous.*" I have to laugh out loud at this. "My, aren't we a bunch of fearful Freds these days," I chide them, with a grin. "Look, you're dating someone who actually eats other people!" they retort heatedly. "How do you know one day soon she might not get it in her head to eat *you*?" I shrug, still smiling, nonchalant. "Because I know my turtledove," I gently inform them. "I trust in her absolutely. She's the sweetest of the sweet that ever was. And she was very well brought up by her people. I'm what they call 'taboo,' you see." My friends sit back, grimly shaking their heads, at a loss. "What you are is out of your mind," they mutter. But I don't hear them, I'm too busy whistling an airy little adoring tune and scratching certain special initials into the tablecloth with a fork.

I go calling on my barbarous sweetie at her lair in a picturesquely shabby part of town. She reciprocates my bouquet of red tulips with a glossy-red present of her own—a kiss of her lips, with their particularly rich savor, their dark-hinting gaminess. While she puts the flowers in a jug, I wander into the side room where my darling practices discreetly the occasional necessities of her diet. I sigh at the crocheted shawls crammed into the fetish cupboard, at the neat mounds of ancient and genteelly threadbare dresses and accessories—all the noncomestible leavings of unwanted great-aunts and grandmothers who constitute my lovebird's staple.

But then I call her angrily into the room. I've spotted the forensics, ill concealed, of another kind of prey. A large canvas bag, of the sort to carry newspapers for delivery, is squashed in behind the radiator. "Dearest, I have told you again and again," I remonstrate, "you must simply lay off the paper-route boys! You cannot involve children in all this!" My lovely gapes at me, and lets out an embarrassed, caught laugh. Then she hangs her magnificent head and clasps her hands in front of her artsy-craftsy, second-hand frock, and stares down at the big, vigorously polished tips of her newly acquired walking shoes.

"I'm sorry!" she stammers. "I *know* I shouldn't, and I hadn't the *slightest* intention, it's just—sometimes . . ." Her voice trails off. Her lip crinkles. I can see her blushing tremendously under her tattoos. I wrap her up in my arms. "There now, there now," I protest softly. "Good Lord I don't mean to chastise you! I understand so well about your special situation. I do, I do," I insist. "After all, I love you, you bloodthirsty lamb chop!" I peer down with gentle firmness into her eyes. "But you've simply got to learn to cut out minors," I warn. "It will land us all in nothing but trouble. People get very, *very* upset about their kids being dined upon, in this culture," I explain. I give her a gentle, admonitory shake. "Understand, savage pippin?" She nods, squeezing her lovely eyes shut, her crimson lips pursed. I bend down and place a kiss on her long, coarse eyelashes. I lift one of her big, glossy-nailed hands to my lips and leave a kiss there too.

Later, we go for a stroll as evening falls. We stop on a rise of grimy paving and gaze off under the unkempt tree boughs at the slow-rising moon. We sigh, arms laced. The weight of her head and its chaotic ringlets of hair is on my shoulder. "You know, darling," she's musing, "you're so wonderfully sympathetic and sweet, about my special atavistic needs. . . ." There's a kiss. "But I just wonder," she goes on, "don't you ever, sometimes . . . don't you *worry,* sometimes . . . don't you ever feel concerned that I'll forget myself . . . with *you*? . . ." Her voice on this last word is low, and sly. Her face is turned up to me, tinged with mischief.

I gaze back at her steadily and smile, the words of an earlier conversation passing for a moment through my head. "My dearest ravenous cockleshell," I reply. "I simply trust you—utterly, and completely. But . . . should you ever desire me that way . . ." I pause, gazing smiling deeply into her eyes. "How shall I say it?" I whisper. *"Bon appétit!"* There's a pause for an instant. Then a great bloom of grins. "Oof!" I gasp, as she squeezes me breathless in her long, festively scarred arms. I squeeze back with all the struggling strength I can muster, until we're both gasping in mutual asphyxsia. We shift about enough in our embrace to allow for respiration, and wreathed in the noise of our laughing delight, we kiss, a long and deep and redolent kiss, of the kind that's termed "devouring."

Bubble Gum

I LAND A JOB AT A SMALL PRIVATE SCHOOL FOR GIRLS, FAR OUT IN THE COUNTRYSIDE. I'M HIRED TO teach mathematics. I'm full of high resolve and keen hopes. The headmistress has crisp, steely curls and wears old-fashioned spectacles. She gives a firm handshake with a broad, extremely clean hand. "And finally, I should note," she declares, concluding her various orientational remarks, "that I know the sorts of difficulties you new young schoolmasters have been prey to, in our circumstances here. . . ." She gives a quiet, adult smile, which I answer with a pedagogically wise, comprehendingly nodding smile of my own. I make a discreet gesture of assurance. "Alas, I'm afraid you'll find some of our very modern girls a trifle intent on havoc," she warns, with a sigh. "But we trust in your maturity. And good luck to you," she adds.

The term begins. Immediately I run into serious trouble, in my early-afternoon algebra class for the twelve-year-olds. A bunch of brazen, gum-snapping buds in blazers set up a regular sugar-and-spice shop in the back of the room. They whisper and giggle unceasingly, and pass back and forth a cloth item that shockingly resembles a pair of candy-striped undies, which they actually lift meaningfully to their pert noses, and sniff. Over this they give me the hot eye and squirm about in their seats, blowing pink bubbles, inching their gray school skirts high up their thighs.

I turn to the blackboard, bug-eyed, blinking. I decide the best policy is to simply ignore them. Vehemently I start to cover the blackboard surface with a vast, quaking thicket of variable equations. The chalk jerks about in my grip, squealing hideously. The room bursts into guffawing behind me. I blush in consternation. All at once I realize I have in fact somehow been scribbling away on the frame of one of the classroom windows. There is a figure staring up at me from the path outside. It's the headmistress. I wave down to her feebly. I lurch around to the room. "Alright, alright—" I mutter, trying to downplay the excuse for rising chaos. I stalk back fiercely with lowered eyes to the blackboard proper. "You want a quiz?" I demand. "Is that it, is that what you want?"

At the end of the afternoon, the headmistress looms up beside me in the teachers' lounge. "I've been meaning to ask you, how've things been going these first few days?" she says. Her spectacles fasten on me. "Oh! Why, things have been going quite—" I cry out cheerily, but the lie stops there, as a massive portion of tea and biscuit goes down the wrong way. For five solid minutes I hack and gasp explosively, thrashing my arms in the air, increasingly purple in the face. "I see . . ." murmurs the headmistress, as she steps out of range, daubing at the bits of salivary shrapnel over her blazer.

After barely two weeks of term, my nerves are in shreds and tatters. I hardly sleep. My nights are ravaged by presentiments of ruin and prison sentences, by a seething brain-fizz of pubescent (sub-pubescent) flagrancies, by hypnogogic underage-underwear study sessions in the shadow of field hockey nets, sessions that degenerate into graphic, giggling collaborations of felony and riot, and always, always the hot, pink pop-pop of gum chewing.

One stark midnight an envelope suddenly appears squashed under my door. It contains page after page of incorrectly done extra homework, all garnished in the margins with crude but astoundingly elaborate anatomical imaginings. The aroma of sugary chicle rising from it makes my head reel. I rush out breathlessly into the corridor. The dim lamplight is deserted. I come back inside and feverishly I tear the pages to bits and flush them down the toilet.

The next night, in the dark hours, unrelenting, a second envelope arrives. It has something else inside. I blink down aghast at the sprig of fine hairs I've shaken out onto the dingy rumple of my blanket. The sprig is tied with a flagrant pink bow. The hairs don't look like the type that come from a head. I swallow heavily. I can guess, mortified, where they've come from. My heart clangs like a jail door. With a broken cry I wrench away up to my feet. "That's it!" I whisper aloud. "I've simply got to leave, right away, at once—to just clear out, like all the others, before something monstrous happens—to my career, my bright hopes—to my criminal liabilities!" I haul out my rucksack from the closet. I stuff in some clothes and beloved, distractedly thumbed math texts, and wise thoughts for new teachers. I struggle into trousers over my pajamas, pull on walking shoes, fling up the window with hectic stealth and clamber over the sill. I hang over the side for a moment and catch a terrifying glimpse of the late-burning lamp in the headmistress's window. I drop with a smothered, awkward crash into the bushes below. Limping, I flounder off across the dark hockey fields, toward the darker, sleeping woods.

A pair of spectacles takes all this in from lamplit curtains. There's an amused, self-satisfied snort. Then a sigh. Then the slow tread of slippered feet back to a table. A broad, very clean hand takes the hank of chicle from the saucer engraved with the school initials, and waves it quickly several times under the owner's deep-sniffing nose. There's a profound, intimate grunt. Then the hand goes back to sorting languidly through its cache of pink ribbons, and its swatches of pretty, striped things, its scraps of shocking drawings.

3.

Domestic Intelligence

Domestic Intelligence

While my girlfriend sleeps, I lean among the bedclothes and gently wiggle loose the top of her cranium. I place the skull part and its ruffled crown of hair carefully on the blanket behind me. Then I edge closer and inspect the contents of my girlfriend's sleeping mind. Bits of cotton candy drift through between her ears, as ever. I smile in affection as a plate of butterscotch follows, from the dinner last Sunday at her mother's. I note the card from the flowers I gave her, for no reason at all, a few nights ago. I murmur an endearment at this under my breath. Now I see a mouth —my own—kissing her good night. The lips loom huge and close and blot out all else. Then a bulge of herringbone appears, from the trousers she bought much too baggy, but which she insists on wearing, with that trademark obstinacy of hers. I shake my head at this farrago of apparel. My lips reappear, for a reprise. They look odd. Suddenly my breath tightens and the sleepy grin on my face goes stiff. Those aren't my lips at all. But I recognize them, somehow. I blink as they offer a lurid, smooching kiss. All at once I place them. They're from that repellent young pseudohipster my girlfriend did some graphics work for last week. I met him when she turned the pieces in and he put on his flirty little act for her benefit. I glare at his hairy upper lip as it slowly dissolves into my girlfriend's new aerobic shoes, thumping away in her exercise class.

I sink back on the pillows, in outraged disbelief. For

a moment I have the fine idea of simply cramming the top of my girlfriend's head back any old way, and letting her wake up to that touch of punitive whimsy first thing in the new day. But I restrain myself. I reassemble her head in proper order, jostling a little perhaps. Then I lie back and glower up into the darkness.

In the morning we have our coffee at our table by the window. "All right," declares my girlfriend at length. "What's it all about? Why the mood this morning?" I shrug lackadaisically. "Nothing," I mutter. "Don't tell me that," she announces. She pushes my paper down onto the table and lays her arm across it. "Come on," she says, with amicable, practical firmness. "Out with it. You've been hunched there in complete silence, radiating ill will. Is it me?" she asks. "Tell me what I've done." I look at her. My jaw sets. "I was just mulling over," I tell her, "why you would be smooching it up somewhere last week with that goateed goofball you did the poster for. That's all." She stares at me. She blushes violently. "Aha," I declare quietly, and I remove her arm from the page and raise the paper. "Who told you that?" she demands. She shoves the paper back down. "You were spying on me!" she exclaims. "No, I wasn't *spying* as such," I retort. "Do you deny it happened?" I shoot back. "No, I don't deny it," she admits, going red again. "But it wasn't anything—he's just sort of—enthusiastic, and he got carried away for a moment. But I told him I already had a boyfriend," she says. "Oh, really, how thoughtful of you," I tell her.

I try to extricate my reading matter, but she keeps it pinned. "But how did you know?" she demands. "Who told you?" "No one told me," I reply, trying vainly to pry her arm off. "Then how did you find out?" she repeats. She elbows my hand away. "I have my nonconventional sources," I inform her. She places her other arm on the paper and regards me meaningfully. "Oh you do," she declares. "Yes I do," I tell her. "Listen, you're getting jam all over the sports section!" I sit back with a sigh of exasperation.

She gazes at me narrowly, cocking her head. A shrewd look plays over her face. "Perhaps now *you* might explain to *me,*" she says, "why you were trying to chew your way through the neck of that half-naked mutant of a florist's assistant, out behind the beach party last Friday?" Now it's my turn to exhibit a deep shade of red. "What do you mean?" I hear myself stammer. I squirm in my chair. "I have no idea what you're talking about," I protest, simulating lamely. My girlfriend nods coolly, appraising me. She sits back, returning the paper its liberty at last. She picks up her coffee. "Don't worry, I know you love me," she says. "Just be advised, there are games two can play at!" She watches me over the rim of the cup, amused. Her eyes flick over my face. They narrow a tart increment. "Did you notice your ears don't quite line up this morning? How careless of me," she says.

EARTHQUAKE

WE'VE JUST MET. WE'RE IN LOVE, THOUGH WE SHOULDN'T BE. BUT WE WANT TO BE. WE SNEAK OFF from work and steal up the stairs to our rented room. We pull back the quilt, hot from sunlight, and we embrace: the bed shakes, the walls shake, the floor trembles back and forth. We lounge back at last on the pillows; the bed goes on shaking, the walls shudder, the washbowl rattles on its stand. "It's an earthquake!" she murmurs. "Is that what we've done?" "Look at that!" I tell her. "The mirror's fallen on the floor but it hasn't broken at all!"

Afterward, when things have quieted down, we try to straighten up the room. We hang the mirror back on its nail. But we're too excited to finish all of it. We hurry down to the front steps and sit there, holding hands and eating oranges and watching the city tidy up. Bells are ringing everywhere. Fire engines clang. We look on in delight as men with hearts on their helmets come running up to where a big truck has turned over, spilling its cargo of love letters into the street.

THE GUN

I BUY A GUN. IT'S AN OLD-STYLE REVOLVER, A LOVELY CONTRAPTION WITH A SMOKED PEARL HANDLE and lacy scrollwork along its complicated barrel. I sit polishing it by the window. A girl walks past on the sidewalk. The gun goes off in my hands. I lurch over backward out of my chair. "Holy *Christ,*" I think, scrambling to my feet, staring up at the ceiling. There's a spectacular hole in it. I grab the smoking gun from where it lies on the carpet and look about wildly and then run over to the bureau. I manage to get the gun hidden beneath some underwear just in time for the angry knocking on the door. "Just a minute!—" I call. I assemble a mild, innocent face, and with this I open the door up.

It's another girl. She holds several large pottery fragments in her hands. She's steaming. "I have just moved in to the apartment upstairs," she announces grimly, "and what would you say if I told you that not two minutes ago a *bullet* has destroyed my favorite piece of china in the whole world?" I blush at her. "I'm sorry," I stammer immediately. *"Sorry?"* she says. "*Sorry* isn't really good enough. Never mind that I could be walking around now with a chunk of lead in my brain," she declares. "This bowl—this *former* bowl—it's—it's irreplaceable!" I squirm in the doorway. "I don't know what to say," I tell her sheepishly. "I'd offer you money. But I'm afraid I don't actually have any right now. I've recently spent it all." "I don't want your money," the girl retorts bitterly. "Why don't I just return the favor, and take something priceless of yours?" she announces.

Without invitation she stalks in past me and sets the shards down on the table and stands in the middle of the room, surveying. "Hey now, excuse me!" I protest. "Naturally," she snorts, "there's nothing in here worth a damn. Alright, I'll take that," she declares, pointing. "No you can *not,*" I inform her. "That little painting is my very favorite thing I own!" "Okey-doke, then I'll tell you what I'll take—Mr. Gunman," she exclaims. She turns about slowly, with a nasty gleam in her eye. "Fair is fair," she says. "I'll take the gun." "You must be joking," I cry. I stare at her extended hand. "Absolutely not!" I tell her. She grins at me unwaveringly. Her hand stays out. I walk glumly over to the bureau, shaking my head. I bring out the gun. My heart constricts at the sight of the exquisite hand tooling and ornamentation. "Thank you very much," says the girl, and she snatches it from me.

"Now wait—now just wait a minute," I protest. "This is all wrong. Look, I'm very sorry," I tell her. "Give me my gun back. I'll buy you something else—somehow—or do something. Anything." "Oh no," she says, backing away with the explosive prize behind her, "I'll take this." "I say no—give it back," I insist. I advance on her. She backs up further. I lunge. We struggle at close quarters. The gun swings up in the air between us. Suddenly it goes off. With a shout we crumple together onto the floor. The girl sits up, gasping. "Well, now we're even," she pants happily, through the smoke. "My precious painting!" I cry. There's a glaring hole in it, right between a pair of plums, beside a bunch of grapes. "Oh, don't look so inconsolable," says the girl. "I have any number of friends who can paint you another just like it. You know," she says, "for all the damage and trouble it's caused, this is a pretty-looking gizmo, I must say." "Give me that," I snarl, grabbing the weapon back from her. She grins. She climbs to her feet and goes over to the table for her china shards. She looks about. "And you know," she says, "really, this isn't such a bad-looking place. . . . When you come to actually consider it . . ." she adds.

And that's the story of our first meeting, all on account of my revolver. One thing turns out to lead on to other, surprising things; that's how these things work, it seems. And eventually we feel inspired to move out of our separate places, and try one together. I present her in time with a handsome new bowl, she keeps her word about a painting with plums. On Sundays, after we've puttered about the house, we take our beautiful gun to the park. There's a secluded place we've found where we like to lie and just shoot at the clouds all afternoon. Or we lie on our elbows with our earplugs in and our fingers entwined on the trigger, and blast our paired initials elaborately into the sides of the green, long-suffering trees.

BAY

I'M OUT ON THE GREAT BAY. HAND ON THE TILLER, I STEER MY SMALL BOAT IN TOWARD THE LOOMING FIGure of the woman on her side, rising out of the swell. I bring the boat into the lee shadow of a monumental thigh. I cut the motor and lash an anchoring rope as securely as I can to the prominence of a knee. I forage in the larder box for the makings of a sandwich, and brew myself some tea for my thermos on the little paraffin stove. Then I jump dexterously across, and scale up the rise of the woman's jutting hipbone, where I take a seat, just above where her hand lies on the top of her thigh. Her wrist makes a convenient ledge for my repast.

I sit for a while with my knees drawn up and my arms clasped about them. Beneath me, the enormous, half-submerged torso slopes away to the shifted mass of a breast, and then to the great sleeping face, one profile forever disclosed to the wind and the clouds, the other eternally buried in the dimness of the waters. There is a kind of gently amused expression discernible on the noble, stony features, as of a dreamer fondly observing her own phantasmagorias. "How many centuries has she lain like this, simulating the deeps of night?" I muse. "How many waves has she smiled at, how many gales driven across her sleeping brow? . . ."

I take up my sandwich slowly and bite away a mouthful. The milky tea is harsh and sweet.

All about me, as I gaze off, spreads the bay in the

last of summer, with its archipelago of prone, sleeping giant females extending to the horizon, like so many grand mysterious isles. I ponder, as I never tire to, the nature of their origins, of the great upheavals of water and rock that created them, in days of geology beyond memory. I reflect on the months I've spent among them, docking in their shelter when the weather turned, clambering over them in the fine days, sitting on their heights at sunset to watch the great ball expire temporarily among them, splashing them luxuriantly with violent colors. Or watching at night sometimes, in a sea of their dark bulwarks, with the full moon unfurling its yellow mysteries among them . . . I have a week or two left of my idyll, before the season closing in forces me back to the mainland. . . .

"Yes, they've been memorable days," I reflect, rising stiffly to my feet. The sun is starting its descent and the wind has freshened. I pull on my cable-knit sweater.

I climb back down into the boat. I run my hand affectionately over its smooth-worn wooden rail, durable and solid. I fill a small pipe and set it in my teeth. Then I untie, and the noise of my engine rumbles against the swell of a giant thigh. I start back out once more on my easy voyaging, my feet braced, the wind ruffling my head, my heart quietly and deeply sustained, as I turn my gaze this way and that to the great sights about me.

Bucolic Days

I HAVE ARRANGED AN ASSIGNATION IN A GARDEN. I SLIP IN THROUGH THE HEDGE. I WAIT IN THE MOONlight, but my beloved doesn't show. Steadily the night air grows more and more voluptuous with its scents of tuberose and quince; the moonlight throws its lazy gilding around me; but I remain alone. At last, heartsore and half-asleep, I sink down dismally and snore beside the flowers.

I wake up fringed with dew. The sun is in the sky. The back door of the house opens and a chambermaid trudges out with a bucket of slops. She gives me a suspicious look, and then grins to herself as she pitches the muck into the ditch on the other side of the hedge. She glances at me sidelong and goes swanking back toward the house, swinging her hips and her pail.

I get to my feet and slouch out into the muddy lane. A robin chirps raucously. A laundry girl comes tramping along, balancing her day's work on her head in a big basket. She winks at me as she goes past. I watch her go. I sigh. I look off in the other direction down the lane, at the long prospect of puddles. I turn and hurry after the laundry basket.

By the stream I lie in the shade of a tree, munching at an apple. Between bites I pour out my heart to the laundry girl—the whole engrossing catalogue of my misfortunes in love—while she kneels placidly on a rock, beating and pounding her fists into the dazzling linens.

Silver Arrows

I TRACK A GIRL I FANCY THROUGH THE PARK. MY LITTLE FRIEND IS HELPING. IT'S SLOW GOING. THE path veers up and down all the time, and the stubby wings my friend sports are in fact just ornamental, so I'm forced to lug him about on my back, so he can keep up. The arrows in his quiver jab me in the neck. I have to put him down repeatedly to make him rearrange things.

But the girl is impeded also. She has bags of groceries and shopping with her. We've gotten close enough once to wound her—but naturally this has had the disadvantage of putting her vehemently on guard.

We labor up a winding woodland section. We've lost sight of her for several minutes. But now my friend gives a shout. "Where?" I huff. "Over there!" he cries, pointing with his little chubby hand. I spot the tawny blond head suddenly against the autumn red and gold of the leaves. It disappears behind the flank of a crest. "I'll cut her off!" I cry, wheeling and lumbering off the path in pursuit. Almost immediately I catch my foot and the two of us go sprawling. Cursing, we hurriedly retrieve the petite silver bow and bright, scattered arrows. We remount and hectically I plod up the steep-angled incline.

We're in luck. We crouch behind a rhododendron. On a bench in a clearing directly below us, the girl has had to pause with her bags to catch her breath. She looks right and left in great consternation. The silvery feathered shaft protrudes from the back of her shoulder. "Alright," I whisper, "this time make sure it's a good shot." "This breeze is kind of tricky," my friend mutters, glancing about with a screwed-up eye as he fits the arrow to its string. Suddenly we whirl around. A figure looms over us. It's a large woman, in tweeds. She grins, panting, leaning on her walking stick. "Hello there," she announces. She beams. "What a handsome child," she declares. She bends forward. "What is your name, little fellow? Are you going to shoot something?" she asks. "Beat it, Grandma!" my friend rasps savagely. "For Christ's sake, lady," I add, "he happens to be thousands of years old! Can't you see we're busy?" I demand. The woman looks shocked. She retreats. We wrench back around. "She's onto us," my friend cries. "She's bolting!" The girl is on her feet, backing away from the bench, looking wildly in our general direction. She turns to flee. "Shoot, shoot!" I yell, jumping up. The arrow flashes wide in the slanting light. The girl squeals and veers, fluttering her hands, and rushes across the leaf-scattered grass. "She's going for cover, over there," I shout. "The pond's back there, she won't have any way out—I'll go around and close her off, and drive her this way!" I make a hectic, breathless gesture. "When she breaks, you get her," I admonish fiercely.

I rush down into the clearing, past the bench and the abandoned, monogrammed shopping bags, and head over along the far side of the undergrowth. My heart soars with the thrill of the chase. I wheel about, and start in, tramping loudly and hollering stentorian endearments. "My sweetest of sweet, my beloved!" I shout. "My permanent rose! My autumn heart's golden apple!" At last I hear her wounded voice, quailing. "Please," it cries from somewhere not too far off. "I confess I do find you (unexpectedly) profoundly attractive, but my personal life has other priorities just now."

"Oh but true love is merciless!" I bellow. "It won't take no for an answer!"

I crash toward her voice with redoubled violent stamping and thrashing. Suddenly there's a clamor in a rhododendron nearby. "She's breaking, she's breaking!" I shout hectically. I come swarming back out into the clearing. The girl bursts into the open not twenty feet away. She leaps across the clearing, gorgeous in full flight in the splendid gold of the afternoon. A whistling flash stuns her in her tracks. She flings her arms out magnificently wide, as if to the dying grandeur of the trees all around her. Then she twists, and sinks down to her knees, and pitches over sideways to the ground.

I come rushing up. I kneel over her. My little friend approaches unhurriedly, a wry, self-congratulatory smirk on his lips. He stops nearby, and we exchange a silent nod of acknowledgment of his archery. I gaze down at the girl. Carefully I reach around her shoulders, minding the brilliant dart there, and raise her up and support her against my chest. The second shaft protrudes its precious-wrought feathers just off center out of her pullover. The shot struck her dead in the heart. She looks utterly beautiful. "Are you alright?" I inquire gently. She blinks up at me, her eyes slowly focusing in dewy radiance. "I don't think I've . . . ever felt . . . this wonderful . . . in my life," she whispers haltingly, with a trembling little laugh. "You know . . . you've always been . . . the only one . . . in the world for me," she adds. "Oh, my darling," I tell her. Our lips meet. We kiss, tenderly . . . deeply . . . extravagantly.

My little friend watches us, leaning on his bow, pink cheeked. He snorts with embarrassment. He ducks his head away, a snaggle-toothed, wincing grin on his childish face. Suddenly he pushes his bow aside, and turns and hoots, and with his pudgy legs bent he shoots a thin, celebratory arc of silvery water out into the afternoon light, over the glorious, windblown leaves.

THE RAID AND THE KISS

IT'S LATE. I'M GETTING READY FOR BED. I HEAR HUSHED, HEATED VOICES IN THE DARK OUTSIDE MY window. I push the table lamp aside and peer down over the sill. In the bushes below I make out a group of practically naked females, mostly young, all wearing headdresses and garish war paint. I listen: I realize they are discussing a raid, on my very apartment. I bring my head back in and sit down, shocked. Conflicting emotions flood me. On the one hand, having naked women rushing about my place is an exciting prospect. On the other hand, I'm not drawn to the idea of a raid as such —being marauded, invaded, physically attacked. It seems to hint somehow at certain dark strains in my relations with women. "And there's the 'property' side," I observe, looking around. "I may not own a lot of things, but what I do possess I'm really very attached to." After more reflection, I decide the best course is to hurriedly but carefully pack away those things that are really most dear to me, and then take what comes. In stealth I dig out some boxes. Finally I sit breathlessly on the side of my bed in my pajamas with the lights off, waiting.

Nothing happens. I get up and creep toward the window to take a look again. Suddenly I scream as the door bursts in, as whooping figures explode through the window curtains. The dimness heaves with big, colored feathers, daubed, sweat-gleaming breasts, nasty-glinting tomahawks. Multiple hands grab me around the neck and shoulders and force me down onto my carpet. Gasping, I start to struggle. Then I think, "What, am I nuts?" I try to relax. "Just no scalping," I protest, into the welter of grunts and shouts. Strange to say it occurs to me I haven't shampooed for a while, so I might have dandruff, and this silly image of vanity makes me suddenly laugh out loud as I'm rough handled. They trundle me up in the carpet, and I'm lifted and carried out the door.

A canoe ride follows. All I can see from my swaddling are a pair of stars, and the topsy-turvy, silhouetted plumage of headdresses, of slim, upside-down arms and elbows lowering and raising as they work the paddles.

I'm brought ashore at last, and unrolled. I sit up dizzily. I'm in the center of fires and tepees. The raiders stand around me, dour, almost naked, nubile, warbonneted. "My God! Look at all this—" I think. A stern matriarch, robed in a splendor of skins and beads, regards me in the flickering light. "Speak," she declares solemnly. She raises a clattering arm toward me. "Tell us, Skin of a Milk Worm," she cries in a ringing voice, "one good reason we might find that we should spare your wretched life!" The bluntness and explicit menace of her demand shock me. I blink up at her. I look about at the grim array of girls. All at once, a libidinous, slightly hysterical bravery starts to mount through me. I climb slowly to my feet.

"Alright," I announce, finally erect, trembling in my pajamas. My voice squeaks peculiarly with nervous excitement. "Since you put me on the spot, I'll be candid," I exclaim brazenly. "All false modesty aside, I think I happen to be . . . a very, very good *lover.* In particular," I press on, "I *kiss,* with extraordinary art, and effect." A lurid, addled grin splits my face. My cheeks are burning red. A hubbub of murmuring erupts around me. The matriarch cuts it off with a sharp hand.

"Prove it!" she demands majestically. She sweeps the half-circle of raiders with a martial gesture. "Choose!" she cries.

I swallow. "Okay then," I murmur, quaking. I survey the field. I single out a slim, chubbily endowed younger one, with slightly crossed eyes and a schoolgirl's sweet, fat cheeks, which immediately turn positively fierce. She wheels toward the matriarch. The matriarch intones her name. The candidate stares at her. She opens her mouth as if to protest. The matriarch repeats her name, forcefully, as an order. The girl grunts and grudgingly slouches forward. She scowls up at me through her overhanging feathers. "Now don't you bite," I warn her. My heart pounds. I push the feathers out of the way and place my hands firmly on the warm, dusky flesh of her shoulders. I lower my head —but she draws back. I protest vehemently to the matriarch. She shouts something and stamps her foot. The girl swings her head back around, her eyes clamped shut.

I take her by the chin and just plunge right in. It takes a while. The first part is slow going, but doggedly I'm able to shove through and then we do a thorough, sumptuous, voracious job of it. Finally I break away. We stand apart, dazed, gasping. "Well?" demands the matriarch. The girl doesn't seem to hear. She rubs clumsily across her goo-smeared face with the back of her blue-striped forearm. Her voluptuous bare chest heaves. She glances in the direction of the matriarch and gives a grudging, swimming nod of her feathers. She goes wobbling cross-eyed back to her place in the ranks on unsteady moccasins.

I am in a state of exultation. My beslobbered jaws ring from their labors. I hear the matriarch declaring my case proved, and my miserable life spared. They will have much use for me . . . she adds. Murmurs swell again. With a grand swing of her robe, the matriarch turns and goes off to her tepee.

"Thank you—thank you—" I pant. I nod and turn about, swaying in place, smiling at all of them as they start to drift toward me. I feel utterly euphoric with relief and narcissistic excitement. "This raid is the greatest thing that's ever happened to me," I think. Tears spring into my eyes. "God, I really *love* to kiss!" I blurt wildly, and laughing with punchy glee, with the sheer overflow of emotion and ecstatic self-disclosure, I just sink down to the ground right there among them. I lean back on my pajama-clad elbows, crossing my ankles at full length in front of me, gaping and grinning up in my light-headed, unabashedly flaunting splendor. Slowly the raiders gather around me, muttering and eyeing me sidelong with narrow, hot-eyed consideration, grinning back at me wary and toothsome through the barbarous trumpery of their headdresses.

Horn

A GIRL IS CRAWLING AROUND DOWN IN THE WOODS. SHE APPEARS TO BE QUITE NAKED. I WATCH HER FOR a while from the porch. Then I go into the kitchen and fill a pitcher with iced tea and rinse a glass and take these down to the woods, where I find a seat on some pine needles and continue my observations. The girl is below me, in a group of birches. She is young, in terrific shape, tanned all over, with a dark, short head of hair. She moves about agilely on all fours, jabbing and digging at the roots of the birches, staring intently. Suddenly she notices me. She springs to her feet and hides behind a tree. She peers around at me, giggling, discomfited. "Please don't look at me," she says in a funny, fluttering voice. "It will make me very upset," she adds. The simplicity and earnestness of her declaration shame and touch me. I pick up the glass and the pitcher and get to my feet. "You know these *are* my woods," I tell her. "And it's not every day I get to see a pretty girl sporting around in the altogether; but I don't mean to distress you, and I respect your modesty, so I shall leave."

Feeling somewhat dazed by my own gallantry, I come back up to the house. I find the binoculars, and blowing off the dust, I take up my position again on the porch, in discreet shadow. She is back at it among the birches. I watch, shaking my head in amused bewilderment as she gouges furiously near the foot of a trunk. Suddenly a rabbit pops out. She pounces on it. I drop the binoculars. I pick them up; with shaking hands I watch her flush two more rabbits and dispatch them in the same fashion—lifting them struggling to her mouth and biting them clean through the neck.

An hour later she comes trotting up my front path. She has on shorts and sandals now, a buff-colored shirt and a knapsack of what was originally the same color. She looks like a big schoolgirl on a hike. She knocks on my door. After a long pause, with a pounding heart I open the door a crack and peer around it over the chain. "Yes?" I ask in a feeble voice, my eyes fixed on what I can see of the dark, wet bulges of her knapsack. "I just wanted to say thank you for letting me use your woods," she says. "And for leaving when you did!" She gives a girlish, reddish laugh that makes me turn pale. "I would probably have done something mean if you hadn't," she explains. "I mean, that's what I usually do. . . ." Her voice trails off into an awkward silence. Her eyelids flutter abashedly. Then all at once, they stop fluttering. The eyes that fasten on me are gaping, feral.

At this point the call of a horn drifts mournful and agitated from somewhere deep in the woods. The girl turns instantly toward it. I get a full-face closeup of the blotched, heavily slung knapsack. "They're calling for me," she says, twitching. "Well—'bye!" She tosses a hurried wave and hefts her burden, and jumps off the steps, and leaps across the lawn, and disappears at full flight into the trees.

At the Neck

I HEAR A COMMOTION DOWN BELOW IN THE STREET. I LOOK OUT MY WINDOW. A GIRL IS STRANGLING A GUY in the light of a streetlamp. He's appreciably bigger than she is, and he struggles and flails with all his might, but she hangs on tenaciously. Finally his body sags to the pavement. I watch her raise her petite, fearsome hands to tidy her hair, and then go briskly off into the night. "That's the third guy I've seen her fix like that," I reflect, as sirens moan tardily in the distance. "She's certainly a load of trouble, that girl, that's what she is!"

A couple of days later, my phone rings. Somehow right away I know the voice is hers. She asks me bluntly if I'd like to meet for a drink. "Now listen," I inform her, "I happen to know all about you, and what it is exactly you like to do." "Oh you do, do you?" she says. "And how is that?" "Because I've seen you in action, Little Miss Chokehold!" I retort, and I explain about my window. "Well!" she says. A mocking note comes into her voice. "If that's your way of admitting you're . . . scared . . ." she says. *"Scared?* On the contrary," I reply, goaded. "What time shall we make it?" After I hang up, I stare out the window. "I must be nuts," I think.

Even so I keep the appointment. But it's hardly a relaxed cocktail hour. I sip desultorily at my spritzer and train my eye on her every minute. She chuckles continuously, as if it's all one grand joke. But I know better. The subject of dinner comes up inevitably. I demur. "So which way are you walking?" she asks nonchalantly as we come out into the evening. "I'll keep you company for a while—or does that prospect frighten the pants off you?" she inquires, grinning. I give a small, stiff nod back. "If you insist," I murmur tightly, ignoring the taunt.

We're in my neighborhood. We proceed. I keep a careful distance from her, and stay alert. I have my chin tucked against my collar. We go several blocks. We turn across an intersection, toward my building. All at once she makes a feint and I gasp and stumble on the curb, and immediately she goes for me. Her speed and strength are prodigious. She fastens on my neck. I feel her little fingers squeezing the oxygen, bubble by bubble, out of my head. Her face is contorted into the lurid grimace of a blood-maddened pet. I bat at her arms ineffectually. Sluggishly I call to mind a piece of secondhand street-fighting lore, and I kick out in the direction of her shins with awkward, dying vehemence. I kick and kick. Suddenly with a screech she lets go. I stagger away, wheeling off-balance into a lamppost. She hops about ludicrously on the sidewalk on one leg. I lumber off swimming toward my building. I reach it and manage to get inside without being tackled.

I slump against the mailboxes, gulping, feeling at the stabbing ache of my neck, blinking at the spots of blood swarming around me in the fluorescent lighting. There's a loud rapping on the smoked glass of the door. "Let me in," cries her voice. "Let's at least say good night properly!" "You've got—" I gasp, "to be—kidding!" The rapping batters away. Finally, there's silence. "Well, how do you want to leave it?" the voice resumes. "Will you call me? Or shall I call you?" "Look, it's nothing—personal," I pant, striving reflexively for diplomacy in the face of such madness. I'm still trying to catch my breath. "But I really don't think—I'm interested—in pursuing our acquaintance—any further," I announce. There's no reply for a moment. Then the rattling revives with a vengeance. I stagger away from the mailboxes and make for the stairs.

A couple of months later I'm startled to see her picture in the wedding section of the Sunday paper. It's an astonishing document I regard over my bagel. The groom is shown beside her: a puny guy, clearly no bigger than she is. But instead of playing carcass in the rice on the church steps, there he stands, erect, grinning away roguishly to one and all, while his new bride contemplates her bouquet with seemly diffidence. The reason for his swashbuckling assurance is bulky and white and ridiculous. I stare out into my room. "The runt is actually wearing *a neckbrace*!" I inform the four walls.

I spot them in a café sometime later, what must be not long after their honeymoon. They're pressed together like a pair of turtledoves at a far corner table. The hero of love sits there with that hundred-thousand-dollar grin still on his face, while his wife coos and bills beside him. I glance over every now and then, waiting to see what happens. All of a sudden a look comes over her. Her little hands twitch out between the wineglasses. They jerk, and lethally spring upward. Their owner strains, going black in the face with effort in the candlelight. But it's no use! The shiny plastic rigging under his chin keeps his skinny neck inviolate. He actually laughs. Apparently the whole business amuses him! He somehow even works his wedding-ringed hand up between her twisting arms, and blows her little tender kisses until the murderous fit is over, for the time being, and she resumes her connubial ways.

Operatives

I'M SHOWN A NUMBER OF PHOTOS OF GIRLS. THEY'RE ALL GRINNING AND ATTRACTIVE. "WHENEVER YOU ENcounter individuals such as these pictured here," the dour, gray figure instructs, "or any of their numerous associates, you are to take steps immediately to sever all contact." I blink at the array of dimpled cheeks and cute, laughing eyes. I look up at him. I give a laugh of my own, in disbelief. "What, you mean girls—pretty girls?" I protest. "But my gosh, they're harmless—they're *wonderful*!" The steely gray eyes glare at me. "That attitude is about the most inane thing I have heard expressed in the course of twenty-eight years of service," the hard, flat voice informs me. I color, swallowing. The gray hands quiver, so the photos in their grasp rattle. The gray eyes lower close. "For your information, sonny boy, these are all highly trained operatives of deceit, suffering, and humiliation!" the voice rasps. I stare at the floor. I gesture with a chastened hand. "But gee, I mean," I exclaim feebly, "I mean, what are we supposed to do—just turn around and run when a pretty girl smiles at us?" "Yes, if you have to, that's *exactly* what you should do," the voice snarls back, its edges lethal over the rattle of the photos.

During the lunch break, I share a bench in a side courtyard of the facility with a fellow trainee. We sit with our paper-bag provisions. I am in a state of bemused consternation. "Jeez, some of these old campaigners are pretty medieval customers," I find myself commenting, in a breach of official organizational discretion. "You know what my guy told me this morning?" I go on, compelled to play out my need to confide, and I reprise the whole unsettling business with the photos. My companion attends with a gawky, somber, slightly wary face. He continues to chew. He shrugs. He swallows with ponderous care. "These instructor guys know what they're talking about," he declares. "They were all once top life-operatives, that's why they're here." "But surely that's *insane,* what he said," I protest, with almost frantic concern. "How can I go through life having to think any cute girl who acts friendly or approachable is in fact out, you know, just to hurt, to humiliate me!" "Yeah, it's tough, it's tough," my companion allows. He makes an attempt at a philosophical gesture with his half-eaten sandwich. "But if that's what they say, that must be the way it is," he says. "Those old guys in there know what they're talking about," he reminds me again.

We fall silent after this. For the rest of the time left for lunch, I sit there, unopened bag in hand, with the disquiet of my thoughts. Around me rise the plantings of gray trees, and beyond, the dark patches of high-security fencing in the distance.

MYSTERIES

I'M AT A BUS STOP. A GIRL IS WAITING ALSO. SHE LOOKS OVER AT ME. SHE SMILES. I SWALLOW. I TAKE a step and reach out for her shoulders and press my face toward hers. She shouts and struggles away. "What do you think you're *doing*?" she cries. "But—but—you smiled at me," I gasp, completely nonplussed. "So what?" she demands. "That doesn't mean I want you to choke me to death with your tongue!" "It doesn't?" I ask, taken aback. "Of course it does not!" she replies. She glares at me. The bus comes. She blows me a loving kiss and hurries up between the doors. I'm in too much of a state of bewilderment to follow. The bus lumbers away, with faces staring back at me.

I walk off in unhappy confusion. "I simply don't understand how this boy/girl business works at all," I think. "I'm utterly baffled. It's all a big mystery to me."

I go into a bistro and sit over a glass of wine at a table. There's a pretty girl a couple of tables away. I regard her sheepishly. She stares back at me blankly, a look tinged with hints of boredom and disdain. I look hurriedly back at my drink. My brow furrows. I examine her again surreptitiously, maneuvering just my eyes, to be sure. She catches sight of me. The character of her expression takes on the distinct guise of a frown. She gives her head a quick shake and looks off markedly in another direction. I stare at my glass again. My heart hurries in my chest. "Now that was just the opposite of a smile if I ever saw it," I think. "So given the disturbed logic of what transpired so painfully a short while ago, this must be the real thing. Even though she's not expressly 'my type,' " I reflect, "not with all that hair and those weird earrings, still who am I to turn down so open an invitation? But—" I confront myself, "*is* this really an invitation?"

I decide there's only one way to find out. I drain off my drink, for courage. I get up. I approach the girl's table at a feigned amble. I stop at the facing chair. "Hello," I announce. She lifts her eyes slowly and perceptibly jars in her seat. "Yeah?" she mutters, eyeing me perplexedly up and down. Without invitation I sit. I gaze at her. She stares back in a kind of wary mix of alarm and outrage. I swallow audibly. Without another word I lean forward across the little table and tilt my head into position, all very slowly, with the expectation every second of an awful and explosively painful termination of my experiment. But it never happens. Our lips meet. I kiss. She kisses back—with passion. Our kiss goes on and on. I become aware of a voice. It's the barman. "Hey—hey!" he's quietly calling. "Hey there now!" I pull away. I sit back panting, wiping at my battered lips. "Listen," I declare between breaths, "why don't we find a cab. We can go to my place, it's got a wonderful view." She regards me scornfully, her chest heaving. "Okay," she says. She pushes a tumbled lock back in place and resets a complicated earring.

Back at my place, we finally take a break. I sit cross-legged with the sheets around my hips, an ashtray in my lap, an elbow on my knee, chin in hand. I embark on my favorite soliloquy. "So there you have it," I conclude. "As far as I'm concerned, it's all an out-and-out mystery. Things that would clearly seem to indicate one thing in fact imply just the opposite. But not always. Or do they really ever? Just exactly how does it all work?" From the pillows, she shrugs. "I don't know," she murmurs. "I guess nobody really does." She feels at a delicate, unadorned earlobe. "You just have to have a feeling about it," she says, "about how it is between a girl and a guy. It's sort of . . . an art. . . ." She shifts the pillows about to get more comfortable. A contemplative silence descends, philosophical and intimate. She gazes at me. She sneers. She holds out her hand. "You know something, I think you're really very cute," she declares, scowling.

Domestic Scene

I AM TURNED INTO AN ANIMAL: A WEASEL. I FEEL HUMILIATED AND SMALL AND STUPID. INCREDIBLY, MY girlfriend doesn't notice when she wakes up beside me in the morning. I sit huddled on the edge of the bed, fixing on her my huge, mournful, brown weasel eyes. "This morning you put on the coffee water," she sighs, and she heads out to the shower.

Of course this simple request is quite beyond me, because of my size and because of my simple-minded digital capabilities. "Oh thanks," my girlfriend mutters with weary sarcasm, coming into the kitchen and finding the kettle on its side on the floor, where I had sent it tumbling with my hapless maneuverings. She slams the fridge door when she gets out the milk.

At the table, she eats her breakfast in silence, dully ignoring me. I sit in my chair, feeling absurdly small and puny in it, with a bit of tail hanging down back. I have nothing to eat, so I fall to licking my paws. "For God's sake, can't you stop biting your damn nails?" my girlfriend murmurs.

I stop and stare at her. Something in me snaps. "You unfeeling brute!" I screech at her, all my woebegoneness flooding into rage. "Here I've been turned into some kind of rodent right under your nose—*and you haven't even noticed*!"

She stares back, dumbfounded. Her mouth is open.

Then her eyes flash. She slams down her coffee mug so that it slops all over the table. "Look who's talking!" she bellows. She grabs handfuls of her large, loose ears. "What about what's happened to *me*?!" she rages.

EXECUTRIX

MY HANDS ARE SUDDENLY ICE-COLD. TO THAW THEM, I STUFF THEM INSIDE MY MOUTH. THE FREEZing flesh adheres to my tongue, to the tissue of my cheeks. I can't get my hands out. I manage to turn on the oven with my feet, and I kneel and stick my head assemblage into its warmth.

Footsteps come up behind me. My girlfriend's voice announces that killing myself that way is no solution to anything. I try to explain my situation, but my hands gag me. She starts tying my feet up behind me. She learned this in class, she explains, they have more successful deaths than I would believe because the professor is so good, he really knows about these things. I pull my head out finally, to try to get across what I'm really doing before she tries anything irrevocable. I twist around and am confronted by the sight of her in scuba gear and feather headdress. I garble a scream into my hands and throw myself to the floor as a harpoon crashes into the oven, missing me by a hairsbreadth. "You little faker!" she shrieks, flinging down the harpoon gun and stamping off to the doorway. "I can't believe you did that, I can't *believe* you'd pull a stunt like that! I thought you were serious!"

I cower on the floor, blubbering and shaking my head and pulling helplessly at my hands. She's still hot as hell. "Shit!" she cries, banging her fist against the doorjamb. *"Shit!"* But then she stops. She squints down at me nearsightedly. "What is that you're doing?" She bends closer. "Oh wow, I didn't notice that! Oh wow! That's really amazing, *eating yourself up*!"

CEASEFIRE
(SENTIMENTAL CULTURE)

I SPOT A GIRL IN UNIFORM. I'M IN UNIFORM AS WELL. I WATCH HER. I MAKE A SUDDEN DECISION, WITH MY heart. I approach, hands open. "Let's declare our own ceasefire, just between ourselves, at least for a little," I tell her. "Though your uniform is the blue of the sea and mine is the green of the pine forest. We're both so tired, aren't we, of this senseless warfare between men and women, this mania for carnage?"

There's a small café I know a few minutes away, where a half bottle of drinkable wine can still be had, if you know whom to ask. I offer the girl one of my precious cigarettes, and we smoke and look out together at the lovely, embattled river. The late-summer sun turns to gold in the surviving leaves of the hillsides. The air is fragrant and somewhat hazy, and melancholy with the presage of changing seasons. The waiter stands off at the grape trellis with his white cloth over his arm, examining the big, spade-shaped leaves and the vista beyond. The girl is young, from a town up in the coastal mountains. She was called up last winter. Her lipstick is not quite on properly, and her teeth are more yellow than white, but she has a wonderful, rude smile nonetheless, and a warmth about her that stirs me. In fact I've just chanced taking her hand in mine, and she's relented to my importuning and the wine, and is singing in a low voice a song very dear to me, when the big guns start up their terrible work again, and the waiter hurries over flapping his rag and squealing for us to go.

4.

PIGTAILS

PIGTAILS

I CREEP UP BEHIND A GIRL, AND TUG SUDDENLY AT ONE OF HER BRAIDS, AND DASH OFF INTO HIDING around the corner. Gleefully, I peep out. The object of my attentions is standing surrounded by her companions, all of them in their crisp-ironed, school-blue smocks. She is gesticulating vividly in my direction and gabbing away and rearranging with nimble fingers the big red bow of the braid in question. Her freckled cheeks are stained with the heat of her indignation. I cover my mouth with my hand, to stifle my guffaw of delight, a delight that spreads its disarming, peculiar flames through me.

Out of nowhere a voice grunts beside me. I wheel around. A woman of my own age glares at me. There is a mixture of scorn and baffled revulsion on her face. "As a man of your apparently mature years," she announces, declaiming the words slowly as if panning for the sense in them, "don't you really, *really*, have more suitable things to do than pull at schoolgirls' pigtails, and run off cackling like a hyena? Don't you?" she demands. I gape at her. I gasp. I start to try to answer, about eternal, innocent pleasures, etc., but all that comes from my mouth is a further sort of queasy puffing noise. I feel my face at once dizzily drained of blood and yet throbbing with confused, crimson shame. Jerkily I manage to sputter out at last the age-old retort of miscreants, to the effect of people minding their own business! With an awkward, idiotic pretence of nonchalance and dignity, I turn and amble away stiffly down the block. At the corner, I glance back and my scourge is still there, staring after me. The girls come trooping into view, and hurriedly gather around her, as if for protection. They all point my way, in unison. I creep off out of sight, pelted with shame.

I slouch home, head down, hands in pockets, brooding on the ways of the world. "So what's the big deal anyway?" I demand petulantly to myself. "So I happen to still enjoy a few juvenile pursuits. So? So what's the harm? It's all part of, well—of my charm—as a character. My delightful eccentricity," I point out, warming to my defense. "My winsome, incorrigible youthfulness!" At this point I come abreast of a shop window, which presents a sudden excerpt of reflection in almost forensic detail. I stop in my tracks, taken aback by the specimen on exhibit before me. It's of a gent with faded hair, and mournful eyes, and a face long past the tender stage. A man, if you will, incontrovertibly toiling in the midst of his lifetime. But toiling in the midst of his lifetime, alas, in the same spirit as someone fallen overboard at sea can be said to be toiling in the midst of the squall-swept, howling ocean. . . . These gloomy observings chill my beleaguered, pigtail-pulling heart.

Eventually I find myself returned, by slow tread, to my front door. I pause on the steps with my key heavy in hand. Two lively young customers make their way along the sidewalk in my direction. They whisper to each other in animated appreciation of mutual scandals and raptures. They see me, and all at once they straighten, to smile at me in tandem, in brash, experimental boldness. But their smiles slowly muddle, and they drift on past me and beyond, glancing over uncertainly, their young brows darkening almost with concern, then almost alarm, at the vehemence of my glaring.

Beanie

"Some broken crockery, a couple of blackened eyes, shouts and curses, lumps on the head—these are all the shiny trophies and badges of ardor at its most marvelous and grandiose. As far as I'm concerned," I explain to a girl. She purses her lips sourly. "Yeah," she drawls. "You're obviously the sort of guy who as a little boy showed his interest in a little girl by pulling her hair." She glances in disapproval toward the bar. I grin. "Now how did you know?" I demand. Her eyes shift toward me. She regards me up and down. "Did you ever stop to consider," she says, "that your emotional development is arrested somewhere around nine years old?" I grin at this even more. I lean back in my chair. "You mean you don't admire my beanie?" I ask her. "My lower-school tie with its little acorns and hammers? My dress gray bermudas?" I flourish a jaunty hand at my lower legs. "My navy blue knee socks?" I exclaim. "You don't find a sort of beguiling poetry in all this youthful finery?"

The girl gazes at me with her chin in her hand. "Seriously, I suggest you consult a brain specialist, immediately," she says. "No, let me correct myself: a *team* of brain specialists, working around the clock nonstop. Working *desperately*." I hoot a laugh, tickled. "How about another glass of wine," I suggest, in a voice lowered to pleasant intimacy, "so we can start on getting pie-eyed and violent?" "No thanks," says the girl. She looks at her watch. "I've got to be going," she declares.

She gets to her feet. "Give a ring sometime," she says. "Whenever you puzzle out another way of being with a girl besides trying to initiate a riot." I reply by thrusting my jaw up in the air. "Come on," I protest sideways along my shoulder, indicating the tip of my chin waggishly, "right here. Right here! Just one little swing on your way out!" She snorts in contempt. She points back at my head. "Your beanie," she says, "has a large hole in it. That must be the source of the leakage." I swivel around. "You can help me patch it up!" I call out as she disappears out the swinging doors. "Ask your *mother,* she'll be happy to do it, I'm sure!" her voice comes back.

I turn back to the table and sit with my drink, grinning if a trifle scarred. "That last crack was an unnecessarily wounding thing for her to say," I reflect, wincing admiringly. "Maybe she's getting the idea!" I peer down my nose at my outfit. I shrug. "I think I look pretty special," I opine. I let out a sigh. I finish off my drink and rise. I edge out from the table and wave to the bartender. He waves back. I feel compelled to go over to the bar for one more look before I head off. I lean on the worn, polished mahogany and inspect the damage while the bartender patiently holds still to suffer the scrutiny. An ugly swatch of bruise has been dabbed under his half-shut, swollen-lidded right eye by a determined enthusiast. I shake my head once more in approval. I give him the thumbs-up sign. He returns it stolidly, and grunts. "Yeah, true love," he admits, as he reaches up to steady the grand cone of his dunce cap.

UNDERSTANDING

I PAY SOME WOMEN TO LET ME ANNOY THEM. AFTERWARD I SEND THEM FLOWERS, WITH A NOTE TO SAY I didn't mean any of my proclivities personally. "Oh, we know you didn't," they tell me when I see them again. "We're used to all sorts of strange things in the amour line." They show me the box of rubber bands they've been collecting for me, the scraps of stiff paper for spitballs. Then they start braiding their hair, because that makes it easier to yank. I sit in the armchair, in knee socks, smoking a cigarette as I observe their preparations. Once more I marvel at the extraordinary understanding women have about men. And what's more astonishing, the compassion they feel even though they have this understanding! I'm going to make it chocolates *and* flowers this time, I decide.

"Well, we're ready," they announce finally. They both have on huge amounts of sweltering clothing while keeping their bottoms bare. One of them is loaded down with suitcases and various luggage, the other has cards and letters to write, a floor to dust, ironing to do. I shift in my seat, wriggling out another cigarette and shivering with anticipation. "Not quite yet?" I ask them. "Can we wait till it's a bit more humid and at least one of you has a headache?"

ANDROGYNY

I'M NO LADY, BUT I NOTICE THE CALENDAR SAYS THE TWENTY-FIFTH, THERE'S A BIG MOON, AND I FEEL A greasy warmth down in the crotch of my pants. I unzip and stick a curious hand in and it comes away bloody.

I go to the bathroom and dig up a tampon from the medicine cabinet. The feeling I get as I strip away the wrapping, as I flick that curious string tail at the end of the cartridge, is disorienting and delicious—a sense of heresy, a surge of infected delight. I bend at the knees, just as I remember they do it, and though there's nowhere for it to go, the tampon slides home. I stand there looking over the empty cardboard apparatus, fidgeting my hips at the foreign stuffing down there, and I'm thrilled. Sexuality is a thread of warp, a thread of woof, and I've gone and tied a knot in them!

The bathroom door slams open. My girlfriend confronts me, hands on her hips. "You asinine son of a bitch!" she bellows. She yanks open her blouse and jerks up her bra. Her gorgeous breasts have shriveled up into nothing.

On Stage

A girl tells me she likes me. "Prove it," I impudently answer back. She gives an elusive, saucy laugh and grins at me askance. "No, not quite," she says. "It doesn't quite work that way." "Oh, and how does it work?" I grin back airily. "Perhaps if we just—"

"Cut!" cries the director. We turn around. The director comes shuffling down the aisle. "What was wrong?" I ask. "Nothing, nothing was wrong at all," he exclaims, waving my complaint away. "On the contrary, it was lovely, lovely. But it's been a long day, for all of us," he says. He has stopped at a seat and grips the back of it. "And frankly my batteries are starting to run low a trifle, so I think we'll just cut right here, where we're so very nicely ahead, and take it up fresh tomorrow." He smiles winningly. "Well, okay," I tell him. I glance at the girl. I shrug. "If you think it—" I break off. The smile has frozen on the director's face. I yell for the stage manager. The girl sinks down in the striped love seat and slowly shakes her head. Her dye job glows with astounding richness in the stage lights. "He's just not taking care of himself like he should," she says. "He can't go on drinking the way he does." "I'm afraid it's an occupational hazard," I mutter, with a sigh.

The stage manager hugs the director under the armpits from behind. "He's supposed to warn me about batteries well ahead of time," he grumbles. "Where am

I supposed to get a special order at this hour of the night?" With a grunt he drags his smiling burden into the aisle and then up the side steps and onto the stage. I help him stow the director in the wings. We prop the leering, ascoted figure against a large tub of flowers from the second-act waltz scene.

"Do you need a hand with the girl?" I ask him. "Naw, go ahead," he says. "There's nothing really to her." I flinch intimately at his phrase, unintentional though it is. I leave him and go get my coat from the dim little dressing room. Before heading off, I look in from the wings for a moment. "Good night, beautiful," I call to her. She looks up past the ear of the stage manager, who is fiddling deep in her chest. "Good night, handsome, see you tomorrow!" she cries with a bright grin. Then her head flips onto her shoulder. Despite myself I gasp. The stage manager turns his head and gives me a nod. I wave a hand to him dejectedly.

I have a late sandwich at the coffee shop on the corner before heading home. Afterward I sit glumly over a worn blue mug. My thoughts keep turning to the girl. Finally I shake myself. "For Christ's sake," I harangue internally. "How can I moon like this over someone who's nothing in fact but an attractive gadget? I must be soft in the head." I pick up the tepid mug and let out a long sigh of distress. "It's time I got out of this business altogether," I reflect. "I cannot spend all my life wrapped up with a lot of dummies!" I stare off bleakly down the street, thumping the table softly with my palm to the lugubrious tread of my thoughts. "Somehow, some way, I've got to get involved with actual humans," I think. "I've got to—the parade is passing by, I'm not any kind of juvenile anymore!"

My Business

I OPEN A MARRIAGE BUREAU. MY VERY FIRST CLIENT IS A WONDERFULLY BEAUTIFUL, OLD-FASHIONED GIRL. Immediately I fall headlong in love with her. It's shocking business practice, I know, but I'm helpless. I manage a couple of desultory, sham sessions with the dossiers of potential candidates, without letting on. But then I just have to blurt out my true heart's feelings. When I'm done, the girl turns her head away slowly without a word. She gazes in silence out the dusty pane of my window, which in my general distraction I've neglected to make spick-and-span for the new season. Outside, obscurely visible, the bushes are thick with fragrant clusters of purple and yellow. Inside, I wait in openmouthed expectancy before my ravishing gazer, my cheeks florid from the disorder of my confession, my heart flapping from my chest toward the blond tresses under her powder blue, green-sashed bowler hat, toward the echoing green of her eyes, toward the mild perfection of her profile above its high collar and clasping brooch. "Well . . . then? . . ." I murmur, in a tremulous voice, when the silence shows no signs of abating. My head and shoulders twitch almost violently. "Won't you—say something?" I beseech, trying to ameliorate my confusion with a crooked little grin.

My client turns slowly back to me. She blinks. For one incandescent moment she gives a slip of a smile. A flame ignites from this and seems to race into every channel of my physical being. I open my mouth to disgorge a torrent of further devotion—but I'm checked by a quick, silencing lift of her gloved hand. Spellbound, as if before an awesome apparition, I watch as she takes up her blue parasol, and rises, and turns, and accompanied solely by the silken rustlings of her long skirt, without a single word walks out the door of my office.

I remain at my secondhand desk for a long time, stupefied with shock and embarrassment. Outside, a couple of birds socialize noisily on a budding branch. Inside, a trace of perfume lingers at my nose. "Gee, I guess I'll never see *her* again," I reflect, wincing, trying somehow to be wry in the midst of catastrophe. I shrug. "She wasn't my type anyway," I observe, now trying to turn to reason for succor. "Too old-fashioned, as you might expect from anyone utilizing a service like this. Almost insipid, really, in an oddly mysterious way! Thank God it ended when it did!"

I drift over to the window, blowing air through my lips, haunted nonetheless by a pair of green, placid eyes, by the demure lushness of a fractional smile. Hands in my pockets I squint out gloomily at the bushes, which seem hung now with a myriad of tiny purple . . . parasols. I curse, and wrench away. "This simply won't do!" I adjure myself. "This is sheer folly!" I come wandering back into the room. "At my stage of life," I continue, exhorting, "I simply cannot afford the luxury of all these seasonal romantic fiascos forever turning my working life upside down. I must, *must,*" I tell myself, "address once and for all my age-old problem: namely, to find a suitable business to put bread on the table." With melancholy determination I start on the task of packing up my clutter of licenses and fictitious testimonials, turning over possibilities in my distressed head, as I labor once again with boxes and string: . . . a millinery operation? . . . a swimwear shop? . . . an establishment for the sale of confections?

STATUE

I FALL IN WITH A BUNCH OF SAILORS. THEY'RE IN PORT ON SHORE LEAVE. WE ALL STAGGER ALONG convivially, arm in arm and drunk under the alley lamps and balcony lanterns. They keep nudging me and pointing meaningfully with their heads at the statue in their midst—an unclad Hellenic fellow they've all chipped in to purchase. I grin back at them, nodding amiably at their prize bobbing above their shoulders. "Yeah, I like art," I tell them. "Music too," I add, referring to the lyre the plaster customer supports in one lolling hand. But then I start to feel stirrings of unease. Something seems peculiar about the whole business, the glints in their eyes when they wink at me. I notice that, despite being sailors, they all have very unhealthy-looking skin.

A group of ladies hail us suddenly from the blazing mouth of an open doorway. They swing their gaudy necklaces and voluptuous boas at us and whoop raucously into the night. The sailors are thrown into confusion around me. They flinch and even seem to blush. Instead of stopping, we veer in a body across to the other side of the alley. "Oh no we don't," I think all at once. "To hell with this!" I extricate myself from the matey arms and push clear a few weaving yards. For a moment, swaying in the lamplight, I regard the lot of them in their whites and backward bibs, with their athletic, tranquil figurehead protruding above them. Then with a large, vehement gesture I turn, and head back over toward the crowded, noisy doorway.

Later, I stand at the window of a room in one of the quarter's numerous particular establishments. "Come on back, mister," whines the girl in the bed. "I'm lonely, here all by myself," she adds. She smiles in the grimy dimness, a heavily rouged, stump-toothed smile. "Just a minute, beautiful," I mutter, without looking over. The curtains tremble queasily in a gasp of late-night air. In the place across the way, the sailors are carousing still behind their own stained curtains. They're all in their skivvies, as they throng about the statue, which now sports a sailor cap over its pale laurel wreath. Their hoots of debauchery spill out into the mire of the night.

ELEPHANTS

I GET DRUNK AND COME HOME WITH A COUPLE OF ELEPHANTS. BUT THINGS JUST TURN AWKWARD AND sloppy and confused, and get nowhere. In the morning the place is a small shambles. It smells. The armchair has a gruesomely dislocated arm, where the ponderous daughter of the pair slumped over against it, trying to balance on her head. I lead my two lumbering, bloodshot-eyed playmates down into the prebrunch street, and pay off a quarrelsome newspaper trucker to haul them back to the circus.

I remount the front steps, huffing and scowling under my hangover. My landlady waits in the doorway, shaking her head. "Besides the noise and the odor," she begins, as I come slouching in past her, "besides all that, those animal trainers have strong feelings about this sort of thing, they're not people you want coming looking for you. I know what I'm talking about," she exclaims. I hold up a hand to her as I start up the staircase, grimly, laboriously. "I'm sorry about the noise, I'm sorry about the stink," I mutter. "I'll pay for all the damages." I tramp on upward, panting, my head a collection of throbbings. "Never mind damages," her voice pierces up behind me. "Please—just go out and find yourself a nice woman your own age. For God's sake, please!" she beseeches.

Acrobats

To impress a girl, I attempt a piece of spur-of-the-moment acrobatics. I fall badly, and break most of the bones in my body. The girl visits me in the hospital, where I lie trussed and prone and immobile. "The doctor says you'll have to be like this for six months, maybe eight," she says, a sad, compassionate smile on her lovely ruby lips, as if somehow to pass as tenderly as possible over this enormity. "But then he'll have you sitting back up, and eventually, maybe even moving one of these limbs of yours!" She looks down at me. There's a moment of social awkwardness, lacking my game reply. But I've lost the power of speech due to extensive nerve and muscle damage. "You just keep those spirits up," she whispers, craning close in a cloud of perfume and patting the top section of plaster-of-paris husk that envelopes me. Her pats resonate in my ears as if I were housed in a great cathedral bell being rung for the holidays. I gape up at her wide-eyed and with excruciating labor manage to blink several times. "Yes, yes, you're going to be fine—fine," she promises, unfurling a grand, warm smile of consolation and encouragement over me. "Just keep those spirits up."

"How's our great acrobat today?" a brisk voice booms, and the doctor bursts into the room. He's young and idiotically good-looking and athletic. "Oh, he's doing—great!" gushes the girl. She straightens herself up abruptly from bedside. The doctor seizes my chart from its holder and scans it and then me and shakes his head.

"Sorry, matey," he declares, with a brawny sigh. "It's going to be a good long while." He thrusts the chart back with a noisy flourish. Then he claps both hands on the rail at the foot of the bed and leans forward. The shadow of his head and shoulders protrudes across my plaster of paris. With intimate gusto he considers first the girl, then me. "I can understand your thinking, sport," he exclaims confidentially, addressing me, but his eyes fixed back on the girl. "A man would want to show off every kind of way he could for such a lady as this. But," he adds, roguishly narrowing his eyes, "you've got to know what you're doing! . . ." He winks. The girl giggles and bites her lip. The doctor lets loose a full-throated whoop and flings back his head prodigiously and shoots out his arms and launches himself backward straight up into the air. The girl gasps. The doctor turns over slowly six feet above us, clutching his knees to his chest. For a moment he seems to hang under the ceiling lights, displaying the soles of his shoes. Then the fluttering white back of his coat appears, then his wildly free-swinging stethoscope, then his triumphant, straining face and white buttoned front as he descends. He lands with a sickening, snapping thud. There's a stunned silence. The room erupts with his screams. "My thighs!" he howls. "Help me! Help me! Dear God—my pelvis!"

The girl shrinks against the bed beside me, crying out into her hands, which are pressed to her face. I gaze in obstructed horror down past the foot of my bed, over the thickened, crusty lip of my carapace. Nurses crowd in alarm at the doorway as the fallen doctor thrashes this way and that on the floor, his limbs splayed out grotesquely beneath him. He bellows in his agony, heaving and floundering, helplessly trying to raise himself onto his shattered legs.

In Prison

I AM PUT IN PRISON. IT'S A WOMEN'S PRISON. I TRY TO DRAW THE ATTENTION OF THE AUTHORITIES TO THIS blatant error, but their response is a distracted grunt and a peremptory wave of the hand, to dismiss me back to my cell.

The iron door clangs behind me. My cellmate is a maniacal dyed-blond creature. At night, when the guards are dozing in front of their television, she slips a silky nightie out from under her pillow, and climbs down softly creaking from her bunk above me. The fuzz of moonlight through the narrow, barred window lightens onto her bared thigh, onto the furtive delicacy of her lifted, naked foot, as she proceeds to disrobe. I glimpse her over the edge of my blanket for a terrified moment or so. I hear the slippery rustle of the nightie as she wriggles it on. Eyes shut, I imagine it like a sheen of candy floss and oil over her. She crouches softly down by my bunk when she's done. She whispers to me to let her in. The waves of scent from her plain-washed flesh flood over me, and my heart batters in my chest, in my throat, out into the squalid shadows of our cell. But I lie with my eyes clenched shut, feigning sleep though she entreats and entices. I have heard the stories of her gruesome history. I know what lies in store for me should I yield to her salacious entreaties. I feel her bloodcurdling fingers on the coarse-woven blanket, but I lock myself in, my arms pressed high, rigid, my own fingers clutching the blanket close. Soon the whispers turn to curses, and then to threats of such hair-raising, intimate brutality, that I hear my own silent voice in desperate prayer. At last, bitterly, my temptress accepts the night's outcome. The bunk above sags. The guard makes his turn along the concrete passageway. After his tread has plodded into the distance, drowsy mutterings filter down from the hard pillow above, to mine below.

When mornings come, haggard, I strive to answer the roll call as if ignorant of what transpired during lights-out. The rest of the prisoners nudge each other as I labor over my breakfast. They hiss at me nasty, mocking things, anatomically coarse things, as if actually delighted by my catastrophic predicament. I blink down at my tray, the off-white bread sticking in my throat like a gob of unset cement. My bunk mate lounges at the far end of the long table, fixing me over her gruel with lewd, predatory absorption.

As always, at our weekly interview, I beseech my court-appointed lawyer to remove me from this monstrous and terrifying circumstance—to correct this terrible distortion of justice and fate. Always, he sighs. He looks pained. He rubs the top of his balding head with hapless deliberation. "Ah, women," he mutters philosophically. "Women, women, women! . . ."

Coins

I own a mansion. However, I go about as one of the gardeners. A peculiarity of temperament is responsible for this. I poke and clip away at part of the lawn, at a few ornate bushes, and do some watering. But much of the time I just shamble about in old work clothes, staying out of the genuine toilers' way. I don't believe the servants quite know what to make of me. On weekends I pay one of the gardeners' women a few coins to let me slip in to visit her in her shack. She smells of boiled rice and cooking grease, and damp earth.

Whatever I'm able to accomplish by this mode of life, it still doesn't satisfy that peculiar yearning deep within me. One day I simply quit the mansion, and hire on with a cargo boat that runs up and down the coast. I'm a rich man, but morning and evening I swab the battered deck for a while. Then I stand leaning on my mop, smoking, watching the dying sun stain the vast sky pale yellow and pink over the open sea. Behind me the shore blackens and becomes its forbidding, mysterious nighttime bulk. The deep yellow eye of a beacon shows now and then from the blackness.

I offer an arrangement to the captain's wife, who keeps the boat's books and manages the stores. But she's a self-important type, full of the dignity of her squalid station. She puffs at me from behind her mildewed counter and waggles her voluminous, tattered bodice and contrives to look offended. I shrug and turn away, stroking my unshaved cheek.

At the next small port, I stay ashore. I loiter there, ruminating in my fashion, tracing with a nicotined finger the water marks on the café tables, wandering the plazas in the late afternoon, drifting down the half-cobbled alleys. Finally I take up with the laundry women, who toil along the riverbank up behind the town. Each morning I go out with them up the rocky, hilly path. I bear a portion of the day's load in a great wicker basket on my shoulder. I struggle along as best I can while they plod ahead, balancing their much grander burdens on the crowns of their bright kerchiefed heads. They never fail to be amused by my presence among them, a man doing such work. But I'm impervious to these sorts of considerations. As the sun climbs, I lounge in the shade, watching them bent over the stones among the piled glossy fabrics. I murmur along occasionally to their work tunes. I pick at a blade of grass, and wonder again why I live as I do.

"Here I am, a wealthy man," I think. "Most folk would have nothing but envy for my station in life. I could buy almost anything, and everything, a person could imagine. So why is it I do as I do?" I muse. "What is it I seek? Is there perhaps some profound want gone unsatisfied from my earliest days?" I pull a meditative face. "They say childhood casts its shadow over the whole of a life," I observe. "Was there, I wonder, some essential consolation that I was never afforded—or on the contrary, yearn to continuously restage?" I think of my childhood. I shrug. I get slowly to my feet and go over to help with the wringing out.

On Sundays I troop out to where one of the laundry women lives. A big tin tub is waiting for me. I put the clump of coins on the little table beside it and undress and get in. The woman rolls up her bright sleeves to her shoulders. Soon her burly arms are all white with thick foam. I lie sunk back up to my ears against the rim of the tub, my eyes drawn shut, while she laughs and shakes her head in the steam, and the warm, damp air fills with the coarse aroma of the crudely made soap.

5.

Dark Hospital

Dark Hospital

I GET A JOB AT A HOSPITAL. IT'S FOR VICTIMS OF LOVE. THE WARDS ARE DINGY AND ILL FURNISHED, and the sufferings of the stricken in their squalor are truly heartrending. I'm overwhelmed. I have to stuff my ears with bathroom tissue to try to shut out the moans of anguish, the cries of longing, the desperate monologues into imaginary telephones that are never answered, never connected. Even semibuffered so, the tears often drip down my chin as I ply my mop sluggishly up and down the worn, crumbling corridors. Sometimes I just come to a halt in my faded uniform, and hang on my mop, and turn my head away, covering my eyes against the sights before them.

One evening the ward nurse heads over toward me all of a sudden as I loiter snuffling over my pail. A gust of anxiety adds itself to the turmoil of my emotions. Her brow is grim. "Will you kindly get control of yourself?" she announces in a fierce, lowered voice. She waits. She shakes my arm. "Will you?" she insists. I nod, gulping. She glances around over her shoulder. She signals a bright hello to a patient shuffling along in the distance. She turns back. "You simply cannot take things to heart like this," she declares sternly, urgently. "We need a clean ward, and an effective, cheerful staff, which means a staff who do not *alarm* patients! Do you understand?" she demands. I nod. There's a pause. I smell the warm, close scent of her perfume. Another gust trembles through me, of a different sort. "I'll be right there, dear!" she calls, into the distance. "And think of yourself," she resumes. "You don't always want to be an orderly, do you? You have ambitions, I'm sure I've heard you talking about them at some time or another."

I stare down at my bucket. I feel the shabbiness of my ill-fitting uniform. "I aspire to be . . . a doctor!" I confess in a whisper. "Well, I don't know about *that,*" she answers coolly. "But there are many kinds of worthy things to be accomplished here among these very unfortunate and seriously unwell souls—*who cannot be helped by people who suffer even worse themselves*! Do we agree?" she concludes. I nod. The nurse pats my arm in approval. "That's *good,*" she declares. She offers a brief, professional smile. "And now *please,* do take all that paper out of your ears!" she pleads. She rubs her hand across her forehead, and with a hyperbolic sigh, turns on her heel. "Here I come, my dear, I'm all yours!" she calls out, heading up the floor.

I watch her go as I stand slowly pulling out the wadded trails of tissue paper. The sounds of the ward flood over me with all their untrammeled lugubriousness. I try to keep her exhortations before me as a rallying flag, but my heart falters. My eyes are fixed on her shapely, stiff-skirted, diminishing legs. I swallow heavily. I turn away, and take hold of the mop in its bucket. I set a wan, strained grin on my face, for the benefit of the ones in their beds. But as I start up trundling among them, my soul trembles, hearing their wretched cries, knowing it's only a matter of time before I'm in there with them.

Contagion

IN A CAFÉ-BAR, I SPY A PRETTY GIRL. DESPITE MYSELF, I CAN'T RESTRAIN STRIKING UP A CONVERSAtion. I make an incautious witticism. She laughs. She laughs again, at another witty bit. Foolishly, I've had something to drink. In sheer recklessness I join her at her window table. We order something to nibble, and we eat, and the laughter continues. She maintains an easy wariness, but clearly she's amused, intrigued. A feeling of dread rises through me.

When she excuses herself to the bathroom, I stare after her. A cold sweat breaks out on my skin. She has incontestably attractive legs. With a groan of horror, I wrench around onto my feet. I dump some money out by the plates and glasses, and rush off out into the dusk. I stagger along, desperate, flapping away the fumes of her perfume with the table napkin I still clutch in my hand. Then I curse and fling the starched cloth away into the gutter. She very likely may have laughed into it, it could be utterly contaminated with her presence! Frantically I rub my hands on my windbreaker. I plunge down onto a bus-stop bench and start lighting matches and waving them about in front of my face. A fat mother and her little son stare at me. I ignore them. In a panic I realize I can still recall the music of the girl's voice, and her laugh, the exact shape of her lips, the contagious sprinkle of freckles on the bridge of her nose. I clamber up onto the bench and squat over the edge and cram my fingers down my throat. The mother and son shout and leap to their feet. I look around briefly at them, quaking from my exertions. They gape at me, pressed up against the pole of the bus stop. "Don't be alarmed—" I gasp, trying to reassure them over the long, gobby streamers swinging from my chin. "I'm just—taking precautions—to protect my health!" I turn away, gagging.

But alas, despite my desperate measures, the diagnosis becomes clear. Once more, I've succumbed: I've fallen in love, all too easily, just like that. I lie bundled up on my couch at home, asweat, twisting about, seeing the girl's playful eyes, the sweetly almost-broken profile of her nose, hearing the torment of her quick, light laugh. I shiver at the memory of ambling legs. Spasms of yearning heave through me, and then give way to a low-grade, consuming ache. The insidious strain throbs along its painful course. I grit my teeth, and gasp in a dull way, and reset the plaid ice pack on my head and the red-checked muffler about my throat.

Mercifully, experience has taught me that eventually, deprived of reexposure, the malady will burn itself out. But it will require quarantine, and hygiene, and vigilance. "Thank God I never got her phone number!" I think, lying on my elbow after awakening in a discomfort of longing in the middle of the night. I blink groggily at the little night-light on the wall, hearing my beleaguered breathing. I begin to muse aloud disconsolately, in the theatrical manner of the chronically unwell in the depths of the small hours. "Will I ever be free of this infirmity?" I ask the silence. "Or will it only end in the fresh-turned soil of the grave? . . . Oh, be strong, my heart," I exhort miserably. "Be strong!" I sigh. I take a sip of tepid mineral water from bedside. I sink back slowly onto the damp pillow, shaking my troubled head, regretting once more the very day I was born, when the seeds of this intimate affliction were doubtless sown, with those first soft, stooping, unforgettable kisses.

PHYSIOGNOMY

I FEEL MOST PECULIAR. I GO OVER TO INSPECT MYSELF IN THE MIRROR. I STARE IN SHOCK. THE FACE before me is not at all the intimately familiar, careworn visage I'm so used to. It's another face entirely—a girl's. I spin around. But I'm alone. I turn back slowly, to confront myself. I retreat a step, holding up my hands to ward off the intelligence of my senses. But there's no doubt about it: the physiognomy that gapes in dismay from the glass has abundant henna-red curls, long black lashes over green eyes, delicately formed pink lips over little white teeth. She's a waitress at the coffeehouse down the street. She's a beauty, I've got a crush on her.

In horrified woe, I drop my gaze and consider the alien attractions of my lovely arms, my legs, the sassy array of my garments. I groan in anguish and lurch away and collapse onto the sofa, holding my gorgeous head in my hands. I toss it from side to side. Then I swivel, and wrench the phone off the hook. Hectically I dial. "Listen, something terrible has happened," I bray melodiously, when a phlegmatic voice answers. "Hey, who is this?" the voice replies. "It's me, who the hell do you think it is?" I exclaim. I identify myself in lilting tones. "Oh Jesus," says the voice. "Don't tell me, not again. Not all over again!" "Please—" I protest, stung. "Please, just come over!" "Jesus, Jesus," the voice mutters.

Half an hour later there's a knock on my door. "It's open," I call out listlessly. My friend enters. He advances slowly onto the giant, dingy throw rug that inhabits the middle of the room. He stops. He places his hands ritually on his hips. "Don't say anything," I warn him, glancing up from my gloomy perch among the sofa cushions. " 'Don't say anything,' " he repeats. He makes a grandiose gesture of blinking. "Are you kidding me? Are you *kidding* me?" he exclaims. "Every two months you turn yourself into some new girl you have a hopeless crush on, and I'm supposed to come by and pat your hand and not say anything, just keep you company till it's over? Is that what you're telling me, Miss Slinky-Sleeveless-Black-Turtleneck?" he demands, on a note of ferocity.

I shut my long-lashed eyes against the heat of his words. "Believe me, I'm the one suffering in all this," I murmur. "Believe me, I don't believe you!" he retorts. He lets out a large breath of exasperation. "And of all the girls!" he mutters, lifting hands and eyes to the ceiling. He trudges over to the overstuffed chair and sits. He contemplates me sourly. I stare at the tops of my knees, my legs tucked up sideways under my white corduroy skirt. He leans forward. "Listen," he starts again quietly. "Seriously now. You can't keep doing this. It ain't healthy." "Of course I know it's not *healthy,*" I inform him bitterly. "Then why do you keep doing it, over and over?" he demands. "Last time it was the little margarita bartender who wouldn't say boo to you. Before her it was that crazy art student who mainly insulted you, before her, that girl who couldn't even remember—" "Alright, alright," I protest. "It's just so *weird,*" he goes on, "so confused. I mean, unrequited yearning is one thing, but to actually—" He makes a gesture of inarticulate summary. He pounds his knee. "It just ain't *healthy*!" he exclaims. In an acid soprano, through clenched teeth, I point out that I've already acknowledged it isn't entirely healthy. "Then why do you do it?" he roars. "I don't *do* it!" I shout back. "It just, I don't know—it just—somehow keeps happening. . . ." My heatedness trails away. "Baloney balls!" he rasps. "Things like this do not *just somehow keep happening*!" He clubs himself again. He lapses into silence, glaring off to the side.

"And one more thing," he resumes, appraising me again dolefully. "I mean, have you taken a good close look at yourself? Don't you feel like a *jerk,* you've still got your old feet and shoes, despite everything!" "Thank you so much for noticing," I whisper icily, the heels of my brown size elevens gouging my haunches. "And I'm sorry," he continues, scowling, leaning forward again, his voice taking on the timbre of fatal candor. "I'm *sorry,* but I have to say this, in spite of—no, *because* of—our friendship. This girl," he declares, "is in fact nuts about someone herself, only it's . . . me. *Me,* not *you.* I'm sorry, but as it happens *I'm* the lucky fella she has eyes for." His fists are clenched between his knees as he speaks. I press a stiffened finger into a sofa pillow, gritting my teeth, as if his words were blows of iron. "It's awkward, and I wish it wasn't this way," he hammers on, "but it is. Pal, listen to me: This is reality talking, and you've got to listen to it! Are you listening?" he demands. "You've got to cut out this *obsession,* cut out these *crazy*—Oh, Jesus," he says. "Oh, Jesus, Jesus—Hey, I'm sorry. Hey—" He gets to his feet. He comes over to where I sit rocking back and forth, eyes squeezed shut, my delicate jaw quivering as the big teardrops hang from it.

"Hey, now," he protests softly. "Hey, I'm sorry, I didn't mean to blather on and on like that!" He puts his arm around my slender shoulders. "Forgive me, dear buddy," he murmurs, "I know you must be going through hell, you don't need me going at you with my two cents!" "I just feel—so—humiliated, such—a damn—fool—" I burble, swiping at the glut of tears with the heel of my hand. "I know—you're absolutely—right, I just can't—seem—to help—" I stop speaking. I blink past my nose at the consoling hand pressing close up on my bare upper arm. "What is it?" says my friend. "Something else the mat—Ow! You're hurting me!" I swarm twisting about complexly to my feet, gripping his thick, hairy wrist with all my pseudofeminized strength. I brandish his hand in the air between us. It's not a man's hand at all: it's quite absurdly a female hand. In fact it matches my own slim, tenacious hand exactly, but for a lack of nail polish.

"You're not—him!" I snarl on tiptoe, up into his face. "You're *me,* aren't you? I mean, you're *her*—aren't you—aren't you?" "What are you talking about?" he cries. "Jesus, will you let go of me, you crazy vixen, you're *hurting* me!" He wrenches free after several heated maneuvers. He staggers off a few steps. He fetches up in the vastness of the throw rug, kneading his wrist. "Jesus Christ, you almost fractured it!" he protests. "What in hell's own name do you *think*—" But he forgoes the rest. He absorbs the sight of my cosmeticized fists, the savagery of my bared, pearly teeth, the seething noise of my breath. His face turns petulant.

"Alright, alright," he mutters. "Jesus, so what? So okay, so big deal, I'm not him, I'm you—I mean, I'm *me.*" He stirs his shoulders and his arms in an awkward, cowed gesture. "I mean, so I'm human!" he exclaims. "I can't help it, I love the big goof, I don't care if he's already got a girlfriend. I just don't care!" His face is hot and red. "Okay, so I'm a hypocrite," he protests. "So you're not the only one. Jesus, do you think you're the only person in the whole damn world with problems?" he demands wildly. And we stand there glaring at each other in accusatory silence, a complicated girl, and a complicated guy, across the throw rug.

Lovers

I FALL IN LOVE WITH A GIRL I SPY EVERY DAY THROUGH THE WINDOW OF A SHOP I PASS. SHEER force of adulation drives me one drunken evening to break and enter through the lamplit show window, to beseech her as she works late behind her counter. To my horror and consternation I discover my beloved is in fact a life-sized, cardboard cutout: an advertisement. The wailing of an alarm breaks into my distraction. Sirens add their howl. I stumble back out the window and halfway down the block before the cops grab me. The big gleaming cuffs snap around my wrists.

I sit for hour after hour in my cell, mooning out the little barred window. If I crane my neck, I can just make out the gigantic, pale, and peeling eyes, the brow and hairline of the very girl I love in my fashion. They stand on the roof of a building down from the prison. At night these features of my pseudoadored one actually glow a gorgeous, watery green and blue. One of the huge, lovely eyelids lowers and stiffly winks, and winks away all night at the gaudy, madcap world. Above, the moon rises and casts its tinsel glow, and the stars, the ones I can make out, twinkle in their tacky, ceaseless, heartrending way. I sigh, and sigh again, and take a last drag of my prison-issue smoke and drop the glowing butt on the concrete floor. Slowly I grind the ember out, shaking my head in a muddle of caged rumination and regret.

My cell mate lies in his dark bunk above me, twiddling his thumbs at the ceiling. He hums the lone half-tune he knows over and over and over, as is his practice every night. He hums, and mumbles adoring phrases to himself. They say he went into a ladies' clothing store with a jug of gas and tried to set himself ablaze on a pyre of summer dresses. A salesgirl, so the story runs, tore the fatal match from him and called the police. He writes long letters to her every single day from here in our barren cell. She never replies. Every night, before he drops off to sleep, the poor soul ceases his humming and bursts out in horrifying, pathetic laughter, at what a desperate pass his heart has brought him to.

SOLILOQUY

I OPEN MY BREAST AND TAKE OUT MY HEART AND LOOK AT IT THERE IN MY HAND. "YOU OLD FOOL," I address it, tracing its glossy, congested membrane with my thumb. "You scarred, abraded and much-battered lump. You ludicrous, hysteric rock." I shake my head gloomily. "What a life of wounds you've led me into!" I mutter, warming to my self-exposition. "What miseries, what humiliations such that I cringe and shrink even now to recall them. What terrors and agonies of jealousy, what sickness as the clock ticks out the killing silence of the telephone—what overstraining, ravenous obsessions with a voice, a face, a way of walking . . . a presence, close to hand or drifting forever away through the leaves in the autumn evening. . . . Oh, what hapless, brief, deluded ecstasies!" I cry. "Then what shocking wretchedness, what madness of rage and ill will! What pain—what pain, you *painmonger*!" I exhaust my inspiration and lapse into agitated silence. I sit, grimly shaking my bowed head over the ugly, ponderously throbbing, incorrigible weight in my hand. For a moment the thought goes through my mind to just fling the damn thing out in the street. I look toward the window. But of course that's all I do. After a while, I part my shirt and press my burden back into its lair. Then I just sit again, staring at the floor, wiping my fingers back and forth on my trouser leg. Then I fold up my hands in my lap, and the only sound in the room once more is the weariness of my sighs.

MOON

I GO FOR A WALK AT NIGHT. DOWN ON THE BEACH, SOME YOUTHS FROM THE VILLAGE HAVE SUCCEEDED in trapping the night voyager in their nets. They scramble out of their boats and drag their luminous booty onto the sand. They clamor around it, exulting, barechested. The moon struggles fitfully in the black meshing, its soft, golden light playing over the torsos and limbs of its captors. The youths display their knives. There is a tumultuous choral uproar as they pull back the net and the moon writhes eruptively to escape. Then a great shout goes out as the first of the crowd boldly strikes in with his blade.

After a time, I wander up closer. The youths drift about silhouetted in the dimmed radiance of their great beached lantern, chewing on torn hunks of lunar pulp. Their mouths and chins glow. One of them offers me a taste of a shining handful. His cheeks are crammed, his eyes glow feverishly, and he pants with heedless elation. I shake my head, scowling. The brutal scene overwhelms me once more, and I turn back into the darkness. From the height of the palisades I look off into the night sky and the chastened host of stars. Below, in the distance, the scene resembles a horde of glowworms scavanging a luminous carcass.

I go back out at dawn. It's chill, the seasons are changing. The site of the debacle has the forlorn aspect of the aftermath of thuggish debauchery. The hacked bulk lies in the tangle of gritty netting, exposed to the foraging sea gulls. It's gray now, its morning pallor. The blotches of its eternally mysterious craters are simply like cartilaginous blubber. Mortal portions of its age-old beauty have been gouged away, torn out, slashed, mutilated. Scorings and burns cover it, from its desperate struggles against the cords of the nets. A broken knifeblade sticks up into the pale sunlight. A sea gull scrambles to find a perch on it. There is a bad smell, and finally I retreat. I feel sick at heart. The waves spill in and surge ponderously up the sand, lifting and lowering the boats that brought in the catch. I stand for a long while with my hands in my pockets, hearing the gulls, trying to manage my bitterness and distress.

ASH

MY HEART HAS BEEN BROKEN. THE SKY TURNS TO CLOUD WHERE I LIVE, AND PAIN HANGS ITS VAPOR IN the air, blotting out the sun for days. Ash begins to fall, like a dim, grainy snowfall. It patters down onto my roof, into my little garden. I sit in the living room, watching with red-rimmed eyes as the grimy flakes pile up, sifting on top of the stands of flowers, over the shrubs, over the new birdbath and the carefully planted citrus trees. "This is truly terrible," I reflect. "I have to clear this stuff without delay. It's corrosive, it will kill off the greenery, eat all and sundry away!" I go out in my scarf and hat and galoshes with shovel and broom. With dreary urgency I heave and brush at everything, but the ash is falling too fast, and I'm too distracted, blinded by my sorrows. Finally I just stand leaning on the broom, helpless, sobbing softly as the acidic precipitation drifts down, gentle and inexorable, blanketing my beloved garden in mounds and tufts, like a macabre picture postcard, far out of season, and dolorous and gray. I can only shake my bent head and weep at what is going on around me, at all in my life that has brought it on. By the crosshatched front gate, a couple of neighborhood kids have brazenly snuck in. They glance back at me with grinning, puzzled frowns as they build themselves a midsummer snowman. Every so often they wince and curse, as the flakes sting their bare, patting hands.

Burial

I LOOK OUT MY WINDOW DOWN AT THE STREET. A CORPSE OF LOVE IS BEING BURIED IN THE MIDDLE OF the sidewalk. It's naked, like a statue. In a frail gesture of bravado and glamour, it wears sunglasses. The attendants lower it with clumsy care down through the torn concrete. Passersby applaud somberly from the velvet ropes. There is a dark, angry hole in the corpse's white chest, where its heart was.

I turn away slowly from the window, my head downcast. Tears drip down my cheeks. I glance into the tinted mirror, but there's nothing to be seen, only the rubble above the sidewalk, the heavy cascades from the shovels.

PALISADES

IT'S EVENING. I GO FOR A WALK ALONG THE PALISADES BY THE SEA. THE ENFILADE OF HIGH, SLENDER palms nods over me. I stop to light a thoughtful pipe and lean reflectively against the scaly husk of a palm trunk. There is a little commemorative cemetery there, hemmed and crowded by rosebushes. Beyond spreads the glossy, gentle sea with its sedate ruffle of froth. A gang of aggrieved women have succeeded in digging up a grave, and are pulling a man's corpse out. Their dresses have an old-fashioned ponderous splendor about them, suggestive of occasions of plush, bygone hospitality. I watch as they drag the somber, dark-jacketed carcass into the pink roses. I hear the savage clangor of their breathing. The mutilation starts and I take out my pipe and turn away. I hurry off furtively. Frowning, shaking my head, I resume my ambulations, pipe back in my teeth. But my heart is troubled. "This everlasting evil business between the sexes . . ." I reflect. "This cursed imperative for vengeance! . . ." A couple of times I stop to gaze back into the distance, pipe in hand. All I can make out above the colored swell of the roses under the sepulchral palms are some hectic movements, here and there, of sumptuously garbed figures. I resettle my pipe and continue on my way. The light grows dim around me through the slender heights and their bouquets of fronds, and I muse and puff, rubbing a thumb over the interior of a hand. Somberly, I trace the course of my love line.

Along the Boulevard

A FRIEND TELLS ME ABOUT A MARVELOUS BROTHEL. INFLAMED BY HIS WORDS, I HURRY OVER TO IT. ON the porch, fanning themselves languorously, are several women I once formed associations with at various times in my life. I regard them in confusion. "Hello there, *darling,*" they call down to me, in a taunting singsong, as if lying in wait for me. "Fancy meeting you here!" They primp themselves at me lasciviously, in unison. They're all enticingly rouged, and wear clinging outfits that salaciously bare their shoulders, offer up the intimate, soft, abundant flesh at the top of their breasts. I color. I hesitate, thinking of perhaps just trying to brazen up the steps to take up their challenge. I start forward, but then somehow I lose my nerve. I retreat, their hooting in my ears.

The next night, I return. I'm in disguise now, masked and cloaked. I even wear gloves, the thinnest of black ones. The tactic makes all the difference. I take each one of them in turn in the darkness. I am an insolent lover, unnostalgic, hard and disdainful, memorable. There is no talking in the curtained rooms, just their terse grunts, their abrupt exclamations, their loosening groans of submission and pleasure.

A week or so later, I meet my friend at a café. "Well?" he says, grinning, his head tilted to one side. "Well, some people have a genuinely perverse sense of humor," I tell him. "Oh, come, one has to amuse oneself," he says. "At another's emotional expense," I point out. "Someone always has to pay," he says. He shrugs. "Really, was it that bad?" he asks. "No. Quite the contrary," I inform him coolly. "Well there you are," he says. He smiles at me. I look at him. He laughs. He presses up the crumbs of his cake with his fork.

"Well, anyhow," he says. "I'm afraid I have to inform you, that after all that, you've already been supplanted in their affections, by a newcomer." Now it's my turn to smile. "And why should that surprise me?" I answer, dissembling nonchalantly. "But how modest and large-hearted of you!" he says. I make a gesture. I look over at another table. "Well, I must confess for my part, I find it quite inexplicable," he says. "Apparently this cavalier, so they tell me, is absurdly fat and has little gray eyes, and brings them flowers and presents, and sings them old-fashioned songs, and when it comes time for *that* business, they all say he's the soul of consideration. A perfect 'elephant of tenderness,' whatever that might mean. They're all mad about him!—but you aren't surprised at all," my friend says. "But this is the *fascination* of these things, is it not?" he declares. And he sits back in his chair, and plays his grin over me.

Fin de Siècle

I REALIZE THAT MY HEART IS THE SOURCE OF SO MUCH MISERY IN MY LIFE, I DECIDE TO TAKE EXTREME measures. I liquor myself up, and in the privacy of my kitchen, under the bare lightbulb, I perform a crude, hideous, but at last successful procedure at the sink, using the big parsley-chopping knife, then a series of soup spoons, then the knife with the short, all-purpose blade. Grimacing in distaste, my hands slippery with gore, I clap up the vile, thudding knob of misfortune in a plastic leftovers' container. The floor around my shoes is splattered with crimson and shadows.

Sometime after midnight, I slink out into the back alley and make my way hobbling fitfully to a small park in the neighborhood. I shake the ex-organ out into the refuse amid some bushes, and fling the container into other bushes a distance away, and dodge off heavily into the broken-lamped darkness. I regain my back door at last, breathing with difficulty, huge icy drops of sweat beading my gray flesh. But no one is following me, no one shouts alarm. Not even a sudden, massively irresistible sickness of stomach can dampen my spirits as I fumble the door bolt closed behind me, and take one tottering, frantic step in the direction of the sink.

The remains of the night are honestly very bad, and so are the next several days. I lapse into a kind of delirium, which is understandable given the profundity of my ad hoc kitchen ministrations. But even as I twist about gasping in my stained sheets, even as I struggle, all multiple thumbs in the bathroom, with my preposterously unsanitary, makeshift dressing—I'm all smiles. My head veers awkwardly in and out of the bathroom mirror frame, but the edges of my double vision radiate a profound, existential beneficence, a quivering halo of joy.

In not much more than a week, I'm back on my feet, good as ever, save for a slight concavity of posture. Also, I've retained a certain pallor, and for a good while, I tire easily. But really, so what? I start dating with almost voracious abandon. My "love life" so-called becomes a scenario of boundless activity—and astonishing brazenness. Whoever strikes my fancy, then and there I make a strolling beeline for her, be she that strange, sinuous gamin spotted slouching on a street corner, be she yonder jet-set haughty, sitting coiffed, cross-legged, and contemptuous at her aperitif. I present what's on my mind with forthright brass. Often, I'm snubbed. Quite often, it's true, laughed at. More than I should care to admit, I'm toyed with. But times enough, I charm, sensationally. I woo with an unearthly impunity, I take unfazed possession of quite a number of souls, I treat more than one with less humanity, alas, than properly I should. I have girlfriends galore, and sooner or later, for their reasons or mine, I move on to others. In a word, sometimes I win all there is to win between the sexes; other times, the word is short, with two brusque letters. Occasionally I'm let down after truly duplicitous, well-nigh pathological manipulations. But listen to me: hear this: It never matters! Whatever succeeds, succeeds; whatever fails, so it fails. *Because I don't feel a single thing!* No pangs, no torments, no soulful wrenchings or yearnings, no disturbing ecstasies, no twining of deepest celestial privacies. Only the invigorations of activity, rewarded by occasional carnal delectations, or else a mild sigh of fleeting annoyance, as if a bug had improvidently flung itself against the freshly polished sheen of a display window.

"How is it you always seem so . . . so nonchalant . . . so eternally possessed of such . . . buoyant insouciance?" my girlfriends will inquire earnestly, wandering the pleasant confines of my living room. (I've moved since my fateful home surgery.) "How can you be that way all the time?" they want to know. I smile at them from the drinks table. I shrug. I go back to mixing cocktails. There's silence as they drift over to the fashionable paisley-on-paisley sofa and settle down, musing, and take up a picture in its silver frame. "Where is this place?" they ask with a frown of puzzlement. "And why do you, who are so quintessentially stylish, keep a photograph of such a god-awful bunch of littered bushes, and in such an exquisite frame?" My eyes light up as I pass the chilled martini glass over to them and ease back against a neighboring cushion. "Oh, something very wonderful once happened to me there," I say mysteriously. They regard me over the lip of their glass. They dart a glance again at the photo. They turn their heads coyly sideways. "Oh! Something to do with . . . *love*?" they inquire, with a probing, worldly-wise grin. I nod slowly, closing my eyes. Then I burst out laughing. I sit there simply roaring my gleeful, pale head off, clutching a pale hand to that place in my slender chest, while they stare at me, completely perplexed, trying haplessly to find the clue to share in my amusement.

PALMETTO

I'VE TAKEN A ROOM IN A BOARDINGHOUSE. IT'S A SHABBY PLACE DOWN BY THE RIVERFRONT. SAD things go on in the rooms about me—morose, even desperate, things, by people apparently bereft of all will, of the last cupful of hope. On several occasions I watch under my parched and cracked window shade as a load covered in a soiled sheet is half wheeled, half carried down the wooden front steps. A black van stands under the dusty palmettos, its back door open.

I find a length of rope coiled on the shelf of my closet with the beginnings of a noose tied in it. The faded initials of the boardinghouse are stamped on it. I complain to the desk manager. "How can you put such things in the rooms?" I protest. "Especially when you know the state of many of the lodgers here?" He looks at the rope. He shrugs. "It comes with the room," he says. "If you don't like it . . ." He shrugs again dully. "You're always free to move," he says.

I consider this alternative. But some curious lethargy has taken possession of me, some distracted spiritual torpor. "I might as well wait," I find myself thinking. "Besides, I wouldn't want to disturb my work. Even though it hasn't been going all that well really." I shut the rope away in the bureau. Then briefly I have a sudden, strange idea, and I take the rope out and hang it as an effigy on the wall. But it disturbs me, and I lock it away again.

I let my beard grow, though I'm not quite sure it

suits me. I smoke the cheap local tobacco off and on. But it's irksome, with the humidity, and the way the stale, gritty smell gets into everything. But in a way this somehow accords with my uneasy lassitude, as I toil haplessly at my labors.

In the rooming house there are a number of women. They're of no particular age. They have a worn, slatternly look to them, and go about without a sense of trying to appear attractive, clad in not much, because of the damp, wearying heat. They epitomize the spirit of the place. In the evenings, after I've given up on work for the day and had a drink, I stand in the open doorway of my room in a limp, rumpled shirt. I pull at the stubble of my beard, as I do for hours at my table, and watch the female comings and goings. I can smell the dingy, miserable odor of food being cooked in rooms. When any of the women notice me, they look right back at me with expressions of dull curiosity, of tedium. I reach an understanding with one of them. "You're such a pretty lady," I fabricate listlessly. We settle on an amount, and I bring a bottle to her room.

"I don't know, I'm just working, trying to work, that's all," I reply, with an uncomfortable shrug, in answer to her question as we sit drinking for a while. I stare at my barely tasted, bitter cigarette. I wave at the smoke. "What sort of work is it?" she wonders, her voice flat and uninterested as she gazes out the window. There's a pause. I admit that I'm a writer. "But I don't want to talk about it," I mutter. "Have you been here long?" I ask. I gaze at the wall, at the shabby bed against it. "It's an awfully sad place, don't you think?" I muse fitfully. "I don't know why I don't move. . . ." The woman shrugs. "Yeah, it's sad, I guess," she says.

While we're on the bed, her pillow feels oddly lumpy and uncomfortable. I pull the rope out from underneath. I fling it angrily into the room.

We sit again by the window afterward with the lamp off, finishing the bottle. Outside, through the dark, drooping wingspreads of the palmettos, the night lights of the fishing boats at the levee rock from side to side. The clanking of a piano drifts up from somewhere from one of the honky-tonks. The woman slouches against the windowsill, humming vaguely to herself as she blinks out the window, her hands lying gracelessly open in her lap. I slump across from her, sighing, disconsolately considering her bare, unattractive foot, where it rests near a tangled loop of rope, which lies on the floor where it was thrown.

Folk Painting

THREE WOMEN SIT IN CHAIRS BESIDE A STREAM AT NIGHT. THEY ARE WEARING WHITE NIGHTDRESSES. They brush their hair. There is an air about them of melancholy, wistfulness. In the woods beyond, an empty coffin lies open.

Far away on the other side of the hill, a man wanders, in my image. He has hanged himself. Mild of nature, he still wears the rope as he searches.

6.

SNOWFALL

SNOWFALL

OUT IN THE COUNTRY, I PULL INTO A BAR. IT'S EARLY AFTERNOON. SNOW HAS BEEN FALLING FOR AN HOUR. I sit and gaze out at it coming down over the highway. A memory has hold of me, tender and woundingly deep. I get quietly off the bar stool and go outside. I lift my face into the flakes and feel them ticking down onto my skin. I hold out cupped hands, watching the flakes slowly start to pile. But the process is too gradual. I go over to a hedge and brush an amount off. I bring it back inside. "Can I have a glass?" I ask the bartender quietly. It's just him and me in the place. He lifts his eyebrows at the sight of the snow. He's a discreet, veteran sort of a guy. "Highball glass?" he says, turning to the rows behind him. "Whatever," I reply. He brings the glass over. I scrape off the fresh snow into it. "Now if you please, some very good whiskey in that," I tell him. "Not what I've been having." He smiles, a bit perplexed. "As you like," he says benignly.

I sit with the drink and swirl it slowly to warm it. I gaze out the window, deep in reverie. I see another latticed window, with another afternoon snowfall. She and I were in college then, we'd been together just a couple of months. The holidays were starting. We were in her room, waiting for the cab to the train station. Our suitcases were standing by the window. She had on her lapis blue dress, one of the dresses I always remember her in. The horn would be honking for us any minute out in the street, but even so, together we lifted up her dress, and made love astride the luggage—one last, hurried lovemaking before our month-long separation back to our families. I remember the pale luster of her hair, her smooth, cool, fragrant-scented skin . . . how utterly and tenderly lovely and glorious she was as she straightened her blue dress at last, with the snow falling beyond her through the window over the holly bushes. I shake my head. I drink the whiskey slowly, with a great lump in my throat. How long, long ago that was, I think. How fresh, how enchanted, those cold days seemed. . . . When the drink is gone, I just sit turning the empty glass in my hands.

Eventually I make a sign to the bartender, to pay. The snow is now falling only lightly outside. The bartender tactfully acknowledges the amount I've left. "Does that drink of yours have a name?" he says, as I'm putting on my coat. I look off, and shrug. "No, not really . . ." I murmur, half smiling in wistful irony at the metaphor. He regards me. He nods. "I hope it helped," he says quietly. I glance over at him. It's my turn to make a gesture of acknowledgment. "If I'm back this way sometime, I'll stop by," I tell him from the door. "I'll try some of that excellent whiskey straight, like it should be." "As you like," he says. "Who knows, maybe by then there'll be April showers." He grins. "I'll bet those make a good mixer too," he suggests. He points with his head at the window. "Go carefully now in that beautiful, cold stuff," he says to me.

PANTRY

"WHY IS IT SO DARK IN HERE?" I MUTTER. I FEEL ABOVE MY HEAD FOR A DRAWSTRING OF A LIGHT bulb. I paw about vainly in the darkness. Exasperated, I curse and rummage through my pockets for matches. I find some and strike a light. I scream. I jerk backward, colliding heavily with the wall. After a stunned, gasping pause, I hectically strike another match and hold up its quaking light. "My God, my God," I moan aloud. The walls of the chamber around me are stacked with the bodies of women, arranged in tiered shelves hazy with cobwebs, like loaves of bread in an abandoned pantry. They are naked, motionless and somber, seemingly asleep. But they're more than asleep. A cold pall mutes them forever, all gray, all lifeless. I scan them, aghast, my mouth hanging open, in the livid flare of the match. It dies. I strike another, and revolve slowly about, flinching, my shoulder turned in, my free hand half raised before me as if to protect myself. I know each one of them. The match goes out.

I fumble back out into the main part of the old house. The pale light of winter afternoon is from another world. Around me the furniture stands forlorn and still in its cloth drapings: a setpiece of emptiness. I drift to a halt by the French windows, and stand, looking out at the empty hills, hearing my labored breath, blinking at the tears. I know them all. Each one of them was once an intimate part of my life. "And now . . . it's all come to this . . ." I murmur, my grief hot on my cheeks. I remain like that, standing in the pale-lit, airless room, blinking and slowly blinking, feeling my whole self dully resound at each muffled stroke of my heart.

HEART

I GO TO THE DOCTOR. HE EXAMINES ME. AFTERWARD, HE REGARDS ME SOMBERLY OVER HIS glasses, across his desk. "It's your heart," he says. "As far as I can tell, right now it's nothing more than a charred, corroded lump. . . . Have you recently experienced any sorrow in your personal life?" he asks. Through my shock, I can barely hear him. I nod, staring at the floor. "Yes," I whisper. My throat chokes up. "Is there any hope?" I murmur, with cracked faintness. I rub the knuckle of a thumb across my eyes. "There's always cause for hope," his voice replies. "But it will take time. Lots of time . . . and much courage. . . ." I nod, head bowed, unable to speak. "Thank you," I manage to get out at last.

I make my way on foot along the street, down to the promenade by the beach. I go along the boardwalk in my overcoat in the sunshine, drawing quavering breaths at edge of tears. I take a seat on a bench, and despite my embarrassment, the tears stream down. I sit sobbing with my chin down on the big buttons on my chest, heedless of the occasional glancing passerby. At length, I collect strength and wits enough to raise my head. I stare out at the waves, sniffing noisily, wiping at my runny lip with the back of a wrist. I think with stabbing forlornness of the doctor's description of my heart. "I'm so damaged and sad," I burble, hearing his words: "charred, corroded lump." "But time—time will heal it," I murmur, in trembling, stuttering cadence. "And courage—" The sound of this word undoes me, and tears pour again. Eventually, they subside. Overhead a gull squawks and wheels. I sit panting, staring out at the sand and the foaming line of the sea, my throat aching, my cheeks stiff, my eyes scalded, my spirit bleak and overwhelmed, beaten to the verge of exhaustion.

In the Snows

I'm up in the mountains, lost in the heavy snows. I struggle in the drifts, woeful, panting in my wool-blanket coat, the sweat growing into clots of ice on the big rim of my hood. Coldness and despair close about me.

I stumble onto a cabin. I pound frantically on the door with my soggy-mittened fist. A weight of snow slumps down from the roof beside me. The door opens and I fall inside.

A girl lives here. She slowly hangs up my clothes while I lie by the wood stove wrapped in a great animal skin. Dazed by the warmth and some food, I blink at her as she moves about. I can almost see right through certain parts of her, as if she were made of glass: one of her cheeks, an ear, the tender nape of her neck, the soft inside of a wrist. She notices the way I'm looking at her. She bends beside me to put some wood into the soft red mouth of the stove. The reddish light glints on her. It makes a fractured play of reflections, and for a moment, an eerie, poignant heightened transparency in which naked bone and sinew are plainly visible. The girl closes the stove door and reaches up to a cupboard. "It's ice," she declares quietly. She brings out two cups. "I was lost in a storm of my own. Like you," she says. "I'm like this since. I'll never thaw. It's permanent." She gives a shrug, and an abstracted, mechanical little smile. "But I'm used to it," she murmurs.

I don't say anything. I turn my head and gaze out

the rimy pane of the window. The snow continues its chill, ponderous progress. The bleak, expiring evening light is slightly luminous because of it. A vast and forlorn country lies out in the massing drifts, and I ponder again with a swell of sadness what brought me to it, and created it as a personal landscape. I lift my hand to the tear that rolls down my cheek.

Later, the girl sits beside me with her tea. Secured in the depths of the animal skin, I quietly recount my story to her, how exactly I came to be hammering at her door. She listens, nodding her head in communion. The lamplight plays across the disfigured areas of her lovely face, the places where once upon a time someone so tenderly set his kisses, before those terrible words were spoken.

Stone Fence

I MOVE ACROSS A FIELD. THERE IS A WOMAN SITTING BY A STONE FENCE. I STOP A FEW FEET AWAY FROM her. "Hello," I say to her pleasantly. "That looks like a good place to be sitting." She squints up at me. "Yes, it is," she agrees. "I've been walking quite a ways," I tell her. "Would you mind or think it odd if I sat down here with you for a bit?" There's a pause. "If you like," she says. I lower myself down stiffly beside her. "Ah, that feels good against the back," I declare. I smile. The woman echoes it carefully. She must be pleasant looking when at her best, but now she's drably clothed, and noticeably large dark areas spread under her eyes, down onto her cheeks. Other marks of extravagant suffering score her face. I'm not surprised when she quietly produces a certificate and holds it out for me to see. I look at it. I nod. "You're not afraid now that you've sat here with me?" she says with a little smile. She tilts her head and regards me sidelong. I slowly shake my head back, smiling mildly. "Not at all," I tell her.

Together we sit in the verge of drying grass, against the sun-warmed stones, looking out over the field. "The sun feels good," the woman says. "Yes, it does," I agree. "I've always enjoyed how a field looks after a plough has been through it," she says. "I like the sight too," I tell her. There's silence. "It would be a fine place to spend a good deal of time," she observes. I smile to myself. I gaze down at a stem of grass. I lift my head. "I have to be going along now," I declare. I look at the woman and reach over and press my hand on hers. They say you can always tell from their hands: hers feels dry and harrowed. "I wish you the very best," I tell her in a low, emphatic voice, "and good luck in all things to come." "And I wish you the same," she declares. She looks at me, smiling frailly, as I get to my feet and dust off the seat of my pants. "Well, so long," I tell her. "So long, then," she says.

When I get down to the end of the field, I turn to wave to her. She doesn't see me, she's leaning back against the warm stone fence with her head turned the other way. I climb over the locked gate and start across the field beyond. As I come to the following gate, I hear the baying of dogs in the distance. I clamber hurriedly over and go along behind the cover of the intricately piled stones. I pause briefly to watch the distant figures hurrying into the field where the woman sat. "I hope she gets away," I think. I turn about, wiping my sweaty face with my grubby, torn sleeve. A grove of trees rises beyond the dirt lane, beside a stream. Before I start toward it, I take the time to rearrange my odious document under my shirt, to make sure it doesn't slip out, and mark the way I've come.

A Day's Work

I'm going through rough times. My life has lost its course. A truck gives me a ride, and drops me off in midmorning by the coast. I'm in farming country. The ocean is close, lying down below the sloping fields. I walk along in the dust and quiet with my jacket on my arm. The road rises, and skirts along an orchard. I pause and lean on the split-rail fence and look down over the apple trees. Off a ways, a farmhouse roof shows. A woman is working in the row of trees before me. She must be the farmwife. She tosses the apples into a big thatched basket on the ground near her. I watch her shift the basket laboriously as she moves along. It's hard going. "Would you like a hand with that?" I call out. "I could use a day's work." She doesn't respond. She can't hear me or is pretending not to. I turn away, and look down the grit of the road. "Alright," a voice cries. I look back. The woman beckons at me to come over.

All day I work with her in the apple orchard. We hardly say much. The sun is strong, but there's a breeze off the ocean. The ocean is there all the time, lying beyond the trees.

We work, and don't speak much to one another at all. At the end of the day, she pays me off, and I get another ride from a truck going down the coast. But I always carry an image of that day with me—of how at lunch she brought sandwiches for us from the farmhouse. We sat and ate in silence, with the breeze drying the sweat on our necks. And how, when she got up to start work again, she told me in great kindness that I might just sit there a while. And I did that, I sat there on that calm hillside, thinking about my life, about its grief and disorder, with the green, calm expanse of the ocean lying below me, and the woman working in silence among the apple trees.

HEAD

I WALK ALONG BY THE RIVER IN THE AFTERNOON. I SEE A GIRL IN THE WATER AT THE FOOT OF THE BANK, below a bench. Only her head and neck, and the very top of her bare shoulders, are visible. She looks peculiarly pale. I go closer. I realize it's not a girl, it's a piece of statuary. It has a noble, vaguely Grecian profile and long, abundant hair. Its eyes are closed fast and it smiles, with the expression of someone told to relax and think of deeply pleasing things. To my astonishment, I realize it's speaking. It addresses me. I stare at it. Suddenly I look up the river and down the other way. But there's no one else about. "How extraordinary . . ." I think. The bench is at hand. I slip down onto it carefully. I take out my cigarettes and hold them up with a tentative waggle. "May I?" I murmur. The statue nods pleasantly and keeps on talking. It talks about this, about that, about the various concerns and insights that occupy a life, big and small, all with the same mild, pleasant smile on its face. Obviously it's done a lot of thinking about many things, and so it's sharing its thoughts. Every once in a while it answers my earnest questions good-naturedly, without making a fanfare of mystery or impatience. It's just there in the shallows of the river, as it is, with its wisdoms, chatting away to me.

An hour passes. Then another. Evening gathers. "It's drawing on to suppertime," I think. "But how can I leave?" I count my cigarettes. I put my feet up on the side arm of the bench and arrange my jacket over myself, and lie there, propped on an elbow, smoking slowly, nodding in agreement or consideration as the head prattles calmly on, smiling, its eyes eternally closed. Over on the opposite bank, a first few lights come on and wobble their reflections in the darkness of the river. A big, pale moon rises, and the white stone head below me glows luminous with dreamy radiance in the moonlight.

CORRAL

I READ A STARTLING NEWS ITEM IN THE PAPER: A DOCTOR HAS DEVELOPED A VACCINE AGAINST HEARTache.

His clinic is far out in the countryside, most of a day's drive from town. After several attempts misdirected by locals, I pull onto his place. The vaccine turns out to be a hoax. "I was just very lonely all the way out here," he explains bluntly. "I figured this was one way I could ensure a steady supply of company. Since you've driven all these miles," he goes on, "why don't you take off your coat and have a drink and meet the rest of the world?"

A varied assortment of folk seem to have found themselves in my position. We smile at each other in sheepish acknowledgment. After a while I fall in with a strapping, appealing young woman, and we find ourselves out on the doctor's rambling front porch. Beyond us spreads a vista of wide arid expanses, with an upheaval of distant mountains. The sun has crossed behind the horizon, and the scrub landscape is flooded with cool, magnificent, violet twilight. "Oh, it's been a couple of years now," the girl confides to me. She adjusts her big, filmy scarf. "And you?" she says. "About the same, I guess," I tell her. We share a melancholy grin, tender and collegial. There's a peculiar quality to the girl's big beauty, I reflect, one that both attracts and bemuses me. She lets out a conversational sigh. "So what exactly does he do out here, this doctor?" she says, turning herself languidly around where she leans against a railing pillar, so her back is to the view. I shrug. "Someone said he's some sort of veterinarian," I tell her. "See, there's a corral down there. I guess he came out here quite a few years ago. Someone else said he does experiments." "Experiments?" says the girl, interested in a nonchalant way. Her manner generally combines becalmment and animation in an intriguing fashion. She turns her large body and gazes down in the direction of the corral.

We make our way through the scrub toward it. The moon is up in a tranquil, splendid sea of stars. Music drifts down after us from the house. We reach the posts and planking of the corral. There are several ponies inside. But they're not horses, I realize after a moment, they have squat stubs of horns protruding below their ears. They must be a type of deer or antelope. One of them comes over and starts to nuzzle affectionately at the girl. "He must be breeding them not to fear people," the girl says quietly. "Look how demonstrative it is!" The animal pushes with eager tenderness at her, as she stoops and maneuvers to accommodate its ungainly muzzle against her neck. I lean with my elbow on the planking, watching the scene in silence. The girl laughs, intimately, touched. I look at the animal's insipid face, at the bewitching, ancient tenderness of its eyes.

7.

Tea

TEA

SOME MEN SHOW UP LOOKING FOR ME IN A TEA SHOP. THEY STAND OVER MY TABLE. "LET'S GO," THEY SAY. I look up at them. There are four of them: big, nasty, hefty-set brutes. I decide it would be unwise to try any physical business. Diplomacy, if possible, represents the best course. "I've just ordered a pot of tea," I inform them, trying an appeal to their sense of personal inconvenience. "Cancel it," they reply. "Let's go." "Really, you should try some yourselves," I encourage them. "They have an excellent selection here, not just pekoes, but also—" "Alright, knock it off," says the thinner one with the hawk nose and dark, bony cheeks. "We'd heard you're a real wiseguy. . . ." He gives me a long, hard stare. He jerks his head. I catch the message and get to my feet without further ado. The waiter comes shuffling up with the pot in his hand and stares at us as we walk out past him.

Outside on the sidewalk they make a tight group around me. The morning is still early and they squint against the fresh, slanting sunlight. The burnt tang of coffee fumes from somewhere intrudes into the air. "So just what is it I'm supposed to have done, to invite all this concern," I demand, carefully addressing the thin one. "You and that mouth of yours," he mutters. "You know the deal," he snarls. "Stay away from these joints, stay away from the brewed leaf and suchlike!" "But what could *possibly* be the harm in my enjoying a refreshing cup of tea occasionally!" I protest, glancing nervously down at the array of big, gloved fists around me. It dawns on me that they are all clutching blackjacks. Someone spits. "Jesus!" I blurt out, realizing what I'm in for. I look around in a panic. There's a sudden, lethal-sounding movement beside me.

I wake up in a hospital bed, in a slowly throbbing, aching daze. My head is covered with bandages, which obscure one of my eyes. Toward evening, a nurse comes smiling into my room with a tray. I bleat in horror at the smoky fragrance of green tea. Clumsily I thrash the delicate tray off my bed, cursing. "Do you want to get me killed?" I screech piteously.

Every late afternoon, at teatime, I have a serving of mineral water instead. The hospital is in the old quarter of the city. I lie propped against the pillows, staring off brooding through my window at the ancient linden tree outside in the soft, deepening, golden light. My nurse appears and turns on the lamp preparatorily and clears my tray. She is peculiar and lovely, and very soon I fall in love with her, and manage to persuade her of my sincerity. She is mute, as are many of the hospital staff. That's how things are in this part of the world. She tries to teach me her sign language, but I'm a distracted pupil. One day she brings in a bright yellow, noisy parrot in a cage. The parrot is her pet and companion. It comprehends her signs and pronounces them into speech for her. Our love affair proceeds as an odd threesome, with the parrot's metallic, squawking voice representing the nurse even in the furtive scenarios of moonlight and bed. . . .

With the arrival of spring, all my bandages are off and I'm well enough to leave. The nurse maneuvers things to come along with me. We rent a flat-bottomed boat and the three of us make a languid voyage down the byways of the great river. It's famous tea-growing country. Whenever we put in somewhere, we stay well clear of the tea shops. We find our way to mineral springs. We sit on gnarled promontories, sipping the bubbly fluid from tin cups straight from the rocks, talking quietly and squawking. The dark, delicate clouds of the small trees and bushes surround us. Wrapped in our cloaks, we gaze down on the ancient brown course of the river as it curves into the hazy, majestic distances, making its way through the overhanging cliffs and flowering mountainsides. The tiny workers move about high up, bending over the little bushes.

"But *why* don't they want you to drink tea? . . ." the parrot muses in its cage, echoing noisily. I sigh, and shrug, as ever. "Who really knows . . ." I reply, stroking my silent nurse's ear. Her head is in my lap. I consider her beautifully wrought earlobe. "Who can ever say what it is, with people like them. . . ." I murmur absently, transferring my finger and my attentions to the black, vivid, arresting brows of her uniquely lovely eyes.

Elm

A WOMAN'S SEX BREAKS LOOSE FROM BETWEEN HER LEGS AND ESCAPES OUT INTO THE STREETS. IT TERrorizes a residential neighborhood for an entire afternoon. A dapper old geezer hobbles over toward it right after its appearance on the sidewalk and makes the mistake of jauntily trying to handle it, and gets a finger bitten off for his presumption. A gang of teenage truants who taunt it in a garden are driven away howling. It flaps and seethes after them, snapping off the sticks and baseball bats with which they try to fend it away. One of the youths relates his terrified drama over the radio, of how he tripped and fell down, and only saved himself by hiding for over an hour in a trash can, while not two feet away in the alley it squatted gnawing on a rusty bicycle pump. Most disturbingly, a dozen schoolchildren on their way back from a museum visit are traumatized by the sheer sight of it. They huddle together wailing and sobbing long after it has disappeared. Every so often a single childish voice still bursts into pathetic screams. The teacher can be heard gasping on the radio in half-sentences. "Tender young psyches" and "in ruins" are phrases she repeats numerous times.

Around dusk the escapee scuttles up into an elm tree and there the authorities surround it. It keeps them at bay, flapping and spitting from the branches. A policeman crawls up with a snaring pole and has it wrenched from his hands. A nasty stalemate ensues.

I listen to the account of all this being broadcast on

the radio. I turn my head. Someone's at my door. I switch on the porch light. It's a bulky, worried-looking man, wearing, in the old-fashioned manner, a hat. He announces himself as a deputy to the mayor. "Can I come in?" he says. I extend my hand toward the room and he steps in past me. I indicate the armchairs. We sit. He gets right to business. "And not only is it a public outrage," he concludes, "but it's only a matter of time before someone loses more than a finger." He grins with difficulty. "And it's a terrible embarrassment to the city, and the mayor," he adds. "Something's got to be done, immediately. You've got to help us." I lean back in my seat. "Me?" I ask. "Why me? What about the woman to whom, how shall I put it, it 'belongs'?" He shakes his head. "She's too distraught," he says. "Well, you can imagine—" He shrugs. "I mean, how would you feel in her position?" he declares, coloring slightly in the lamplight. I don't answer. He leans close. "Listen, we all know your books down at city hall," he says, an intent look on his face. "We're big fans, we think you have a special understanding, a facility, about these"—he makes a vague motion with his hands—"sensitive matters. That wild story about all those la dies washing themselves," he says. "And that other one, about those wigs up a—"

"Then you'll also know full well that I've just gone through a tremendously difficult and disabling time, won't you?" I interrupt. I get to my feet. I walk over to the mantle. "I'm in no position to have a relationship right now," I mutter, my back toward him. "My God, no one's asking you to have a *relationship*!" he protests from the room behind me. "We're simply asking for your help for just one evening." I don't answer. I stare at the mantle. "Please," his voice beseeches, from closer behind. "We're desperate. You're the only one we believe can save the situation. Think of the innocent people—the kids," he adds. I roll my eyes at the hyperboles. "What is this, some grade-B cop thriller?" I mutter. "What's that?" he says. "Nothing." I sigh. I close my eyes. I rub my hand over my face. I let out another sigh. "Alright," I murmur, "alright, alright." I turn blearily toward him. "It'll take me a few minutes to get ready," I tell him.

In the bathroom, my hand trembles as I shave and then find the old cologne bottle and the jar of pomade. I take out my dark blue suit, the one I always look good in. I still do. I give my brown-and-white-striped tie a last tug in the mirror and shake my head with a grunt, at the ripple of memory and melancholy. "Alright, let's go," I exclaim somberly, reemerging. "To do this one hundred percent I'd normally stop off for a boutonniere, but we don't have the time."

Our official car maneuvers through the police blockades. We turn a final corner and the scene is in front of us. Squad cars and fire trucks pack the end of the street like a disorganized mass of cattle. A couple of spotlights are trained into the upper branches of the elm tree. A fire ladder probes the forbidding, leafy darkness. Its rungs are empty and ominous. The crowd, the curious and the frightened, strain from the barriers for a glimpse of melodrama in the red, slow flashing of the squad-car lamps. It's a circus, a bloodletting, a zoo with cage doors broken.

The deputy explains to the police chief who I am. The chief holds a big red handkerchief to his nose against the faint, celebrated smell of fish in the air, as we walk hurriedly along. "This is what I want," I declare quietly, my eyes fixed on the locale in the branches right above the ladder. "I want this entire street cleared, I want each damn one of these spotlights off, I want nothing here but this ladder truck." "You must be crazy!" the chief barks through his handkerchief.

"There's no way I'll authorize anything like that. Do you realize what could happen if—" "Listen," I snap, swinging about. "I do this my way, or I don't do it at all." There's a stark pause, taut with stares. "Do what he says!" the mayor's deputy cries. "Do exactly what he says!"

The chief swears and turns away. He starts to shout blurrily through his bullhorn.

Fifteen minutes later, the street is empty. There is only the elm and the ladder from its truck, and me, and the moonlight. The black hulk of the mayor's deputy's car watches from the end of the block with its lights off. I take a breath and look up along the diminishing metal parallels. I whisper good luck to myself, wet my lips, and start climbing. The only sounds in the street are my steps mounting one after another from rung to rung through the dark branches, and the lilt of the ballad I'm whistling. My eyes are fastened on the ladder top. From above the growing saline aroma sends down a ripple through me. I press slowly on. At last, without incident, my head and shoulders clear into the zone of high leaves. The scent in the moonlight is tangy and unadulterated. I pause there, clutching on and whistling now in a tender, ultra-intimate tempo. The melody tugs soft and piercing at my heart, as I smile right at my quarry, crouched not more than a couple of feet away, in the saddle of two branches. It resembles an innocent head of hair of a young brunette child. Streaks of exposed wood gleam pale near it, where it has gnawed away the bark in its fits of temperament. Slowly, gracefully, I exhibit an open hand to it, with fingers relaxed and slightly spread. "Hello there, you beautiful oyster," I whisper huskily. "I know you and your kind, you moonlit kitten, you pretty sea muffin . . . you sweetmeat with your pride of fur still on! So pretty, so pretty," I coo, as I reach very gently forward, and touch it.

Lightly I begin stroking, employing just my fingertips. The mons veneris feels tense, dry. I continue this nerve-racking procedure for several sustained minutes, alternately whispering and whistling. The soft, plush hair sends a throb through me. I blink away sweat. I swallow, and start to feel about delicately for the little pink knob. I find it. I commence my attentions there—gently, gently, just with the soft pad of a fingertip. I feel the muscles begin to relax, and then the first moisture. Fresh waves of pungency rise over my head. I tremble powerfully at them, and lean close, and slide a finger into the cleft. The lips turn immediately slick. I work away there, then back to the knob, feeling the spasms of response. My breath grows hectic. I grunt, in labor, and involuntary appreciation. My wrist is starting to ache. I wiggle up awkwardly another rung, so that I'm several feet well clear of the ladder top. With a flutter of trepidation swampy with desire, I slip my hand away as deftly as I'm able, so both right and left can grip the ladder. I bend forward. "May I?" I murmur in a thickened voice, as my heart throbs through me, and I lower my mouth. The old taste is briny but sweet, almost fruity, like melon and seawater. My tongue finds the little knob right away. Expert as ever, it worries it. I maneuver about with increasingly firm, fervid, lingering strokes. Memories flood me. I plunge my whole face down, shoving my tongue deep into the sloppy cleft. I rub with my nose and shake with my cheeks and work my tongue to a fare-thee-well. The object of my attentions bucks around under me. The ladder starts to sway and dip as the two of us go at it for all our worth, up among the leaves and branches, under the gaze of the moon. Suddenly my balance goes, and I burst away and hang on wildly as I swing outward, and then treeward, on the ladder's swiveling pendulum. I throw back my goo-plastered head and laugh in abandon and intimacy up through the greenery, up at the blinking stars. I manage to stabilize myself at last against a branch and I give a clearing pull over my face with my hand. "Come on, you angry, oceanic mouse," I whisper to it, smiling in all tenderness. "Time to go home. . . ." I extend my dapper arm. Slowly, it climbs onto my wrist. It mounts waggling up my sleeve. I feel its sopping heat through the material. It perches finally on top of my shoulder. I start down as carefully as I can on wobbling legs, laughing gently as my burden nuzzles my neck. After a couple of pauses for rearranging along the way, I step down at last onto the bed of the ladder truck and then, finally, onto the street. The mayor's deputy's car rolls slowly toward us. . . .

Sometime later, the car turns onto a street of brownstones in a different part of town. "And thank you again—for all of us," the hatted figure calls quietly through the window, as I start to mount the steps to a front door. The car pauses, then drives off into the night. I watch it go. I ring the doorbell. After a few moments, I hear hurrying footsteps. The door jerks open. The woman gapes at me. Then she cries out and in her emotion, covers her mouth with her hands. "Everything's fine," I reassure her, "everything's fine." I present my shoulder toward her. She reaches out with both hands and seizes the warm, plump epaulette. I make a gesture of understanding, for her not to concern herself at all with ceremony. She turns and hurries into the house. "Please come in, I'll just be a minute," she cries back.

After closer to thirty minutes, she finally reappears, smoothing her dress over her thighs. She's tidied herself up nicely, though she's obviously still feeling great emotion. She comes partway into the room, and then she halts. She lifts her hands, but at a loss, drops them. "How can I ever thank you?" she says. Her face is colored deeply. She rushes up to me and embraces me. I pat her back in empathy. "What can I get you to drink?" she says, stepping back. I shrug. I name something. She goes over to the sideboard and fixes two of the same. I take my glass from her. We sit. I keep my jacket still buttoned. We clink and sip. There's a pause. In the silence she grins with awkward emotion. Her gaze drifts down to her lap, and she laughs suddenly, shaking her head. She looks at me. Her eyes sparkle. I smile back in labored pleasantness. I put my drink on the coffee table. I rub one hand with the other. "Listen, I'm afraid I feel I need to say this," I slowly declare, my eyes on the table. "Please understand, I was very glad to be of help, and I hope, I truly hope you know I had a very, very lovely time." I prod the drink coaster with a pair of fingers. "But I'm still recovering, you see, from a very difficult situation of several years' duration," I explain, "and I'm still not whole. I'm in no position right now to get involved. . . ."

The woman gazes back at me, grinning, a mix of strong emotions working her. "I understand," she says huskily.

I stay awhile longer, and then she sees me to the door. We embrace warmly without speaking. "Good-bye," she calls out softly after me, as I go down the steps. "Good-bye," I call back. I start up the street. The moon is still out and I decide to walk. The night is cool. I turn up my jacket collar. I sniff at my fingers for a moment, and snort quietly, and sigh deeply, and incline my head against the tide of memories as I make my way along through the sleeping town.

GLACIER

I WANDER IN THE MOUNTAINS. I FIND SMALL BUT COMFORTABLE LODGINGS IN A TIMEWORN BUT PICTURESQUE *gästhaus* in one of the lesser localities. From here I make my forays, tramping up the high short valleys to lunch on a steep hillside. I eat my cheese and rough bread while the breeze cools my uncovered head, and amuses itself by warbling across my ears and flicking about my once-abundant locks. Beyond me on every hand rises panoramic grandeur, all swollen with the pride of its lofty granite faces and ridges, its dazzling draperies of snow. I trudge back down desultorily in the pine-scented sunshine, my legs and lungs pained and invigorated, at my nose a bouquet of little snow posies gathered from the midst of lichens and rocks.

At the onset of each day's evening, I write detailed, absorbing letters under the slanting beams of my room. The day's spindly mementos bloom in a glass beside me on the table. More often than not, I will have to put my pen down before it reaches the signature, and cross again to the window, and stand there regarding the day's leavetaking. The village lies dimmed in shadow around me, while high above, the grand arrays of the famous peaks receive their last golden, majestic burnishing, like the triumphant strains of nature's daily symphonic finale.

Later, after supper, I take up, by lamplight, the literary project that has occupied me off and on for some time now. I make fresh notes and interpolate incisive revisions, with a sober clarity born of mountain air. Until my yawning simply won't be denied, and with a sigh I cap my pen and blow out the lamp, and go to the window for a last survey of the rich, frank abundance of the night sky above the glimmering promontories. And so, satisfied, to feel my way back in the dimness to the rustic comfort of my feather bed.

A week or so into this sojourn, I chance upon a peculiar, cryptic item in an old guidebook to the region. Among the quaint particulars listed for the area, there is this squib of "historical" exotica: the site of a girl trapped in a glacier. I raise the issue with my proprietor. Oh yes, he assures me, the girl in the glacier was once a well-known attraction in these parts. He recalls viewing her himself once, when he was a child. But, he shrugs, people have lost interest in such things these days. . . . "But she's still there, visible, in the ice?" I ask. He smiles and scratches his head. Why yes, no doubt, visible from a distance, he would think. He corrects the guidebook's somewhat inscrutable directions for me.

A couple of days afterward, when the barometer promises particularly fine weather, I set out on my pilgrimage. A full morning's clambering up a hidden northeastern valley brings me to the foot of the ice field. I start out onto it. The glacier begins as a narrow, hardened lip of darkly translucent spill, then expands wide as it climbs toward a thickening up-and-down horizon of snow and murky, rippling ice. The going is awkward, and there is a brooding air all about, an almost palpable foreboding, as if at a dangerous intrusion. After almost an hour of uneasy slipping and clutching, I descry the rusting parallels of the chains that mark the old vantage point. I work my way to them. The topography drops off immediately beyond, and then begins to mount again, forming a kind of dramatic if slackly shaped crater or ravine. Across this declivity, in the slanting, gray ice wall of the crater, a figure is patently discernible. The sight is so shocking that I greet it by gasping out loud. Tears of something akin to horror spring to my eyes. But then I find my composure, and I study the spectacle before me, after first tossing toward it the bouquet of mountain flowers I've brought along, as prescribed by custom.

The figure of the girl is poignantly small, and twisted at an odd angle from me, so I can't discern much of her beyond the blackened scoop of her bonnet and her dull, blackened, billowing farm dress. Her arms appear disposed outspread and almost behind, in an ungainly, wrenched attitude, as she were half rushing away in off-balance, girlish alarm, half falling and floating, as if in a dream, through the three and more stories of gray murk that constitute her world. There is something at once absurdly commonplace about her, in her bonnet and farmgirl frock, and yet vastly forlorn, almost horrifying really, in her isolation, her overwhelmed, loomed-over, geologic solitude. There are no archival accounts, I muse, of who she might be; nor of her mystery, how she came to be enveloped here in the glacier, which after all proceeds in minuscules over the course of centuries, of the life of the world itself. No, her situation is a great impenetrable enigma: since anyone can recall she has always been there . . . the girl suspended in the ice's cloudy wall.

I regain my lodgings well after dusk. I'm exhausted, but I sleep little on my feather bed. My imagination is on fire. The image I've borne down with me from the frozen meadows expresses exactly, it seems to me, the nature and character of a certain momentous presence in my own emotional history—a particular person, and a knot of circumstances, the story of which has long lain inaccessible within me, defying description. But now, having gazed down over rusty links of chain at that distant hoary wall, I believe I've found my vitalizing, illuminating symbol.

In the morning, I shove aside my previous foolscap labors and set to work on fresh paper. All day while the sun waxes bright and splendid outside, I darken pages in my room. By evening, I'm completely addled. The sentences have come in gushing torrents, but turbid and chaotic, shifting this way and that to a veering, feverish compass. In the lamplight I scratch out everything I've done, vehemently, heroically, and block out a new course for the following day. But the next day brings more of the same. I work with feverish application, but somehow things bog down, essentials elude me, or choke and overpower me, leave me exhausted somewhere else entirely from where I had projected. I am swamped with reawakened memories and recollections, but in the manner of an observer literally buried headfirst in the rubble of his data. Paradoxically I feel gripped by an almost febrile sense of being on the outside of things, of scraping and grappling and clawing in vain to gain access, to find my way in. The sensation is so derivative of its subject—so quintessential of the difficulties of my craft—that sometimes I have to pause just to laugh out loud. But it's a wretched, wincing laugh, more like a grimace.

This jumbled frenzy continues for several days more. Toward a full week of it, I'm worn out entirely, and in a state of groggy desperation. I feel topsy-turvy, disoriented, continuously overwhelmed. I force myself to take a whole day's respite from table and paper, up into the green craggy hillsides. I eat my cheese and bread, and feel the wind and gaze once more on the peaks and their snows. On tiptoe I try to spy a telltale glistening in what I guess is the direction of the glacier;

but to no reliable avail. I turn around finally instead and look where to pick a frail mountain bouquet.

This tactical secession produces no change whatsoever. And there will never be a change, I begin to realize. That little dark-bonneted figure caught eternally plunging away in her frozen habitat, far up at the end of a hidden valley, too aptly expresses the fate of a certain part of the history of my life . . . of a person, and a tragedy. . . . I put my pen down all at once in the middle of a clogged page, and stare unmoving through the window at the fading, glorious light.

I return to my former ways and tasks. The proprietor is cheered by my reappearance at the public table, although he detects an acquired note of melancholy in my spirits. "It's ever since you went to take a look at the girl in the glacier," he observes, inclining his head and smiling shrewdly, as if pronouncing a subtle country commentary. "Yes, you're absolutely right, she's done it to me," I tell him, with a sigh, to humor him.

Resumed, my literary work of long-standing goes along quite well, and the writing of letters once again stakes its claim to the presupper hour. But I find, quite soon, that the locale has run the course of its appeal for me. Suddenly, I would be elsewhere. I conceive an appetite once again for seas, and balmy beaches, and the undulations of palm trees in trade winds. Overnight I pack up my couple of suitcases, collect and secure my papers for passage, and in the morning, ask for my bill. I take a last tramp up the steep hillsides before I go, for a valedictory lunch. But halfway along, bagged sandwich in hand, breeze in my hair, I lose interest somehow. I turn back, bothering only with the mementos of a couple of plucked flowers, and on this note, I take my leave of the mountains, and their icy, obdurate mystery.

8.

Golden Age

Golden Age

I HAVE THE GOOD FORTUNE TO DIE AND COME BACK TO LIFE DURING FAR, FAR BYGONE DAYS OF A GOLDEN age. I find myself in the palm-crested precincts of some balmy South Seas isle. The locals are as benevolent as you could ever hope, physically glamorous and culturally on the simple side, and spotlessly clean of person. They amble about colorfully half-dressed all day long. I spin out my sunny hours padding the fern-bordered paths with them, bumping down coconuts and bananas to munch as I laze by a waterfall, where rainbows sprout their multiples in the misty, floral air. At night, while the waves rumble drowsily along the pale beaches, the beautiful island daughters come traipsing through the moonlight to my lean-to. Here they yield up their firm, gold-skinned treasures with a laughing generosity that turns this one transmigratory voyager's throbbing brain to syrupy, honeyed fizz.

In the light of morning, who should awaken the two (or three) of us but—of all people!—the parents in question, come calling with bowls of fragrant native cocoa. Scarlet hibiscus blossoms glow on the ornamented cane trays with which we're served. We choose each a blossom and exchange it with one another, in the local fashion of acknowledging the pleasantries of the night just passed, and the breezy, crowded shadows of my lean-to grow merry with good-natured, happy laughter.

So the weeks and months pass, and I count myself

the luckiest and happiest of men, and eminently satisfied with the chancy deserts of being reborn.

And one afternoon, lolling by a luminous pool, I fall into a reflective mode. My favorite young companion of all bathes herself close by in the greenish, orchid-crowded water. Her brilliant sarong lies folded beside me. I sigh, and ask myself . . . isn't there something I can do, as a token of appreciation to all these wonderful folk, for their hospitable, almost mythic, generosity (especially the young females)? A gesture, moreover, to ennoble my state beyond the shameless spectacle of puerile smut, of ultranarcissistic/*über*-adolescent male wish fulfillment. My pondering eye lingers over the bent golden arm and deft, splashing hand of She-Whose-Laugh-Is-as-Lovely-as-the-Blossom-Opening-beside-the-Lagoon.

"Laughing Blossom, darling," I address her, chin in hand. I pick at the nodding spindle of a fern. "Might I inquire on a personal matter, of a fairly delicate nature?" My companion turns her jet-draped head and fixes me with solemn, beautiful eyes. "But of course, dearest Funny-Balding One," she replies. I clear my throat. "Well," I begin, demurely but directly. "Does the word 'orgasm' mean anything to you?" My bather blinks at me. Her lovely brow creases slightly, as she considers. "No, beloved," she announces finally. "It doesn't." I nod in confirmation. I suspected as much. "Well then, allow me to discourse on a thing or two," I declare. And I explain to her how she and her people inhabit a period of time that is truly prehistory—arcadian, yes, indeed, but also profoundly *primitive.* Primitive, that is, in the sense of an acutely intimate anatomical innocence. Laughing Blossom—and all the rest of her sisters young and old in this enchanted early world—is as yet quite unequipped, so I've noticed, with that little strategic *bud* so instrumental to an evolved woman's satisfactions.

"Here, perhaps I can illustrate," I tell her, beckoning her over. She wades across to me and peers down at the half-shell oyster from our lunch on display in my hand. "Now you see this pearl here, that I almost cracked my tooth on a while ago?" I explain. (Pearls are commonplace in these waters; I have a sackful stashed away in my lean-to.) I roll my fingertip over the tiny bauble of silvery slime. "Well, many, many eons from now," I inform her, "a person from your marvelous branch of the species will be born with something like one of these automatically. It's true!" I promise. "Go on, feel it yourself." I coax my lovely to replace my twiddling fingertip with her own. She looks bemused. "You know how at times during the night," I go on intimately, "I enjoy myself so much I just have to shout out loud?" She looks at me. She breaks into a grin. "Yes!" she exclaims. "And then you make a mess over everything and roll your eyes all the way back in your head, like this!" And she mimics me extravagantly and hoots with jolly laughter. "Yes, yes, well," I reply, coloring. "*Anyway:* it's all because of intense pleasure, you see. *And what I'm trying to tell you,*" I press on, "is, by way of thanks for all you and your kind have done for me, perhaps I could take it upon myself to try to monkey, as it were, on your behalf, with the natural pace of evolution—via a bit of gynecological jerry-building I've been turning over in my mind, supply the means for all of you to experience extravagant bliss for yourselves, *right here and now*!" My beauty gazes at me, grown silent once more and full of grace. "Oh my beloved!" she declares quietly. "How good and generous a man you are, in your heart!" And she rises up and presses her face into mine, and gives me a long, nursing, warmly floral kiss.

The next day I seek out the vigorous old crone who passes for the shamanistic personality in local society. She hears me out on my notion, and then stares at the ground, stroking the long hairs on her chin. Finally she looks up with shrewd, narrowed eyes. She nods slowly and grins. "That's one hell of an idea," she says.

The morning ensuing, I guide Laughing Blossom into the old dame's lean-to. The ubiquitous extended family is kneeling outside among the fronds, bearing mashed fruits and semifermented beverages to distract hostile gods. I press my little heroine's hand to my lips as our Dr. Frankenstein goes out back to where a tethered piglet squeals. The squeals turn suddenly frantic, and the pseudosurgeon reappears with my inspiration, a bloody, tingling nub of tail, in hand. "Trust me, darling, it'll all be worth it, trust me," I whisper, as my dear one twists against me, and flinches, and then yelps in pain. The fishbone needle begins its grafting labors with thread.

For the long nights that follow on, I nurse my pioneer through her feverish hours. I soothe her clenched brow with a cool, hibiscus-scented cloth. I tell her stories, to lull her, from that former life I recall through a blurry, interstellar haze. I marvel again at her fortitude and dignity, and her loveliness, both spiritual and of the flesh. "A genuine worthy ancestor . . ." I muse fondly. By the end of the week the fever breaks, and the old crone slowly undoes the palm-leaf bandages. She retires to the discreet distance where the family keeps its vigil, out of sight but discernible by murmured chants of prayer.

I smile down at my beautiful monsterette. I stroke her brow. "Ready, brave one?" I whisper, and I lift her hand down to between her legs and set her gently to making history. She winces. She stares up at me. She winces again. Then she gives a little gasp, and her eyes widen, and she starts to wiggle. Suddenly all at once she throws her arms around me and thrusts her tongue deep into my throat, and when I finally get clear for air, I hold her in my embrace, laughing in her ear, as she bucks and rubs against me. "You see, you see," I murmur, stroking and patting her back, "now you see what I mean?"

The weeks consequent on our isle are a veritable festival of modification. The old crone becomes a very wealthy woman indeed (so many grateful families), requiring the services of a trio of assistants. The pleasant air rings with the frenzies of piglets being chased down through the undergrowth. And I wander among it all with the pride of an honored guest who, having received immeasurable bounties at the hands of his hosts, has discovered the means, via a clever titbit of philogenic fiddling, of repaying their favor.

"Ah me, indeed, what a glorious world it turns out to be, this second time around!" I reflect, as I make my way languorously toward the waterfall where my Laughing One awaits among rainbows. I bear a warm, hairy coconut in my upturned hand as a puckish, self-congratulatory emblem of my sovereignty over happiness. And yet truly, why shouldn't I indulge in a stretch of congratulation? The trampled pathway leads down through groves of ferns, where squads of young lovelies are scattered in the midday shade of the banana fronds. Their hands ply away under their dazzling sarongs, as they wriggle and wrench around. Seeing me, they steal a moment from their salacious exertions to wave to me, and blow me aromatic kisses. And I receive all these with a gentle raise of my hand, and a smirk of modest pride—for my tiny, felicitous intervention into history, and the swelling eons and eons and eons of bliss for which—who's to say not?—my gesture of gratitude may be the very seed in fact responsible.

ISLAND

I'M LOST AT SEA AT NIGHT. THE HEEDLESS, VIOLENT WAVES SLAM ME OVERBOARD FLAILING AND SCREAMing, and whirl me aloft in spectacular catapultings and hurl me down at last onto the grainy shock of land. From its zenith the next day, the sun goads me awake. I struggle to my feet. I go staggering along a beach. The empty sand stretches into the distance and disappears behind a hazy jumble of greenery. Palms lift their stiff, clattering umbrellas into the vast scorching blue. The surf paws languidly at starfish and driftwood. "I'm marooned!" I blurt aloud into the silence, gasping along, fumbling at the mess of dried blood on my forehead. Suddenly I sway to a stop. Through the glare of the sun I blink at the two figures above me on a blossom-spotted rise. They wear little blue caps, and gray skirts, and white knee socks. "Schoolgirls—" I stammer. I lurch a step. "I must be in paradise—" I sputter. "I've washed up near a girls' school!" Squawking, hollering chaotically, I lumber up through the foliage toward them. But there's no sign of them when I've finally slipped and clawed to the top. I stagger this way and that, frantic. I bellow hoarsely among the gaping flowers. But then it comes over me what's taking place. "They were a mirage . . ." I realize, mumbling to myself through dried lips. My heart sinks away in me. I droop there trembling in the sun. I stare down from the knoll at the appalling, splendid kingdom where I've fetched up. The enormous sea closes in everywhere. A cold tremor drifts through me. I sink down heavily onto my knees. My compacted shadow sinks with me. "Well, mate, it's you and me," I whisper to it, with a hollow laugh, displaying a grisly trinket of bravery. I clench my fists feebly and try to rouse myself. "I'll just get through these first couple of nights," I insist, swallowing, "and then I'll make myself a shelter out of branches and vines, and I'll find a spring, and live off nuts and berries. . . ." My voice trails away. Big drops fall in slow, dark sequences from my shadow's poor, distorted brow. Two shadows appear beside it. I raise up my head, disbelieving. "So you weren't a mirage after all," I whisper. I squint up at them, feeble and smiling. They stand gazing down gravely at me, under their flickering monogrammed caps. I sway on my knees. "Tell me, lovelies," I pant. "Tell me, what do you call this island?" They tell me the name. My shoulders slump. I nod, somehow smiling still. "Of course . . ." I whisper, nodding as their white socks flicker. I manage to turn my head to the side, in anticipation, as the waves storm along the beach and foam up through the palms and the bushes and the opened flowers, and swarm over me, and the brutal sea takes me at last.

The Sadness of Sex

I SAIL THE FARAWAY SEAS IN MY BOAT. A SQUALL COMES UP WHILE I'M EATING A SANDWICH. I TRY TO finish the whole thing, gobbling, before making for the beach on the near horizon, but then a nasty gust broadsides my little vessel, and then snatches the captain's hat off my head and flings it out into the waves. I curse and throw the sandwich in after and lurch hectically for the oars. The sea rears and menaces at me. I struggle at the oarlocks, twisting around for the sight of breakers and land. All of a sudden the boat heaves straight up in the air. One oar wrenches loose and goes tumbling away. Shouting, clutching at a gunwale, I am driven along at a crazy, upslanting angle through surf, and then spun completely about, and walloped headlong onto grainy beach. Rain drums down, and the tide crashes and rushes over me in a seething carpet. Stunned, I find my feet and clamber groggily to where the boat is and drag it a few yards up the beach. Then I stumble on to a nest of palms and sprawl down under their shelter.

The squall passes in a matter of an hour. The sun reclaims the blue sky and sparkles on the waves. I sit combing the sand from my hair with my fingers. I am bemused. I am more than bemused, I am a man enchanted. Fortune, it appears, has cast me up in its rude fashion onto one of the loveliest and most peculiar places anywhere on earth. All around me in the lush shrubbery, cottage-garden purple foxgloves and yellow buttercups and bright orange pansies loll under the grand, nodding, tropical palm fronds. The now-tranquil breeze stirs a fragrance my way, a scent not only floral but almost redolent of—I sniff—of toffee. And there is a sound, trembling at the level of hearing, as of a harp being strummed. I gaze off toward the distance where a green, majestic headland towers over the creamy hem of beach.

Suddenly a bird darts out into the foreground nearby. It hovers over the bruised, upturned hull of my boat. I give a little exclamation of delight. It's a bluebird! I follow its course as it flits back to the leaves. The leaves break open, and I gasp: a face peers at me. It's the face of a girl, the face of a big, magnificently pert, overgrown fairy child. It has gray-green eyes and a peculiar, topping thatch of ginger-colored hair. It's the most enchanting, whimsical face I have ever seen in my life. My heart floats right away and instead of its beating there is the harplike music. I sink back slowly onto my elbows. I start laughing. The girl blinks and considers me from the leaves.

"Are you a madman?" she inquires gravely. I shake my head. I swallow and try to compose myself. "No," I assure her. I gaze up at her, beaming. "Well, perhaps, who's really to say . . ." I allow, in a murmur. I make a vague, explanatory gesture in the direction of my boat. There's a pause. "You're staring at me," the girl informs me. "Who are you?" I ask her, sitting up propped on my hands, still grinning unashamedly. "And what might your name be?" "I'm part goblin," she announces, with a note of hauteur. She turns her head to the side and extends a finger over the little crown of the perching bluebird at her broad ear. The top of the ear is conspicuously pointed. "As for my name . . ." she continues. Her gray-green eyes narrow disapprovingly. "You're still staring at me," she says. "I know," I reply. My grinning is uncontrollable. I feel light-headed, dazzled, as if my blood had been turned to dew. "I can't help myself," I explain. "You see I've never met a real-life fairy before." "I'm not a fairy," she scowls. "I'm part *goblin*." "Well, whatever you are," I declare, "I want you to know that I believe you're the most enchanting person I've ever met in my whole life." I halt for the moment with this pronouncement. The girl colors and drops her eyes. She grins, nonplussed. Through the lilting, reverberant half-music my voice continues. "And you should understand," I inform her, intimately, "that I've fallen in love with you at first sight. You've ravished me utterly. I'm completely under your spell!" There's an astounded, harp-loud pause. The girl stares straight down, wide-eyed. Then gradually she lifts her head. "You're very *forward*," she announces, wary and clearly delighted. I sink back once more on my elbows and close my eyes and shake my head, left and right, and send out a laughing peal of joy into the daffy, motley foliage, into the sweetened musical air and blue skies, into this delirious tropic, this shipwrecked, elfin new world with its fantastical, adorable enchantress. The bluebird rises and flutters its wings noisily in midair in consternation.

So my idyll begins. I can still see every bit of it in my mind's misty diorama, as I sit with my cheek inclined on my hand . . . the cottage under the rosy bougainvillea by the brook, where she led me after together we propped my buckled boat against a dry-dock palm; the feather bed below the handmade motto, "God Bles This Cozzy Connir," in which we lay that first night, she buttoned up demurely to the throat in her flannel nightshirt, as softly we kissed for minutes and minutes on end in each other's arms, and inhaled each other's warm breath after snuffing out the candle, and woke every hour, it seemed, to gaze, transfixed with mutual delight, into each other's gleaming eyes; and the gaily painted, ornamental ledge where the bluebird kept his neat, twittering abode. . . .

I can see still that workroom full of pots and hammers and woodshavings and clay, where in her blue smock and beret she fabricated her toys, the toys she transported for sale (now jaunty in her red sugar-loaf hat with white owl feather) to the tourist village inland over the hills. I can recall, prodigiously, the salmon-and-purple hulk of the flowering cabbage, and its court of prickly cacti, which she maintained just because she felt a mind to, among the stands of daffodils and pale pink gladiolas in the cottage garden in the back. I can remember, so the pangs of intimate detail wound me still, the packets of boiled sweets she fancied in particular . . . or turning geographic, those pools where the harsh, tangy watercress grew, which we picked and covered up in checkered cloth for our picnic lunches. . . . There we go, basket in hand, settling down before a sea vista, just at the cool edge of shade (not one for bikinis and suntanning, my elfin fellow-picnicker), on hollowed rocks that were a celebrated local attraction, because the breeze noodled out a delicate cadenza as it passed over them (the source of my come-ashore harp music?), and we ate to this serenade, and the bluebird fussed itself a perch on a hydrangea blossom nearby. . . . It's my own voice I hear, après these déjeuners, reading aloud from the gilded, mildewed pages of a Victorian women's novel, while the volume's owner, my audience, lolled and snoozed at my knee, and then woke eventually, twitching, from the droplets of seawater being tipped, by the mischievous instrument of a leaf blade, onto her snoring nose . . . and then idling slowly back, hand in hand the two of us, munching the last of the gingersnaps beside the opulent, flamingo sprawl of sunset, with the bluebird darting overhead along the foamy sea's edge, until we'd sigh and stop to lace our arms, and press into the weight of each other's presence, and feel loving head incline against loving head. . . .

Such poignant abundance of memory does regret lovingly maintain. Such a wounding wealth of detail. . . . Again it's my own voice I hear, with its endless teasing gambit, "So this is what fairies are like!" just to provoke her eternal, embattled response, "I'm not a *fairy,* I'm part *goblin*!" ("I know," I whisper, "on the side of your maternal grandmother, and what a credit to your forebearers you are!") Or her sudden pidgin questioning of me, eyes sleepily narrowed, in the midst of a late-night saucer of custard for her sweet tooth, "What you laughing at?" and my utterly tender, adoring reply, "Why, at you, oh, rarest, bewitching nincompoop of my delight—at you!"

Or nostalgia, piercing, retrieves that afternoon I come in to find her banging a large nail in beside the mantel, from which she hangs a big wooden mallet with coarsely frayed striking ends. Painted daises adorn the head, twining about the three elaborate gold-and-green initials of emergency. " 'S.OS.'?" I inquire, as the bluebird alights on this new site for roosting. " 'The Sadness of Sex,' " she announces, crossing her arms and fluttering her eyelids in self-conscious dignity. "It's a time-honored implement of protection," she declares, "for a young woman of a household, such as myself, should she be dishonorably regarded. By an older gentleman of the world," she adds significantly. She lifts her nose in the air and eyes me across it in an old-fashioned, grand-mannered way, a sturdy, eccentric, scrumptious version of a girl, in a modified antique housecoat. A gust of purest transported affection almost rocks me back on my heels. I sweep her up in my arms, the bag of sweets I've brought for her still in hand. "You saucy, *violent,* magical goblinoid *chuckle-head,*" I exclaim thickly in her peaked ear, and she gasps and has to struggle for breath, and at last manages to turn the tables, and laughing, lifts me clean off the ground, as the bluebird hops in the air about us, as ever, in protestation. . . .

I wish it were thus forever, a goony idyll in a goofily tropical cottage, with a creature of impish endearment, with me forever returning along the splash of the sea with a little paper-bag gift, eager and certain to be enchanted anew. But alas, fortune (another word for "life," I guess) somehow doesn't seem to care for idylls; and it remembers this one began with a wreck. . . . When is it exactly, I ask myself, that the relentless diet of the picturesque begins to turn a trifle stale? When does it dawn that any pleasures of sex (speaking now in all intimacy) will always be oddly difficult, only occasionally lustful as opposed to affectionate and even nondescript; that the sounds of boiled sweets being cracked between back teeth in the darkness, as a regular conjugal aftermath, will prove abiding cause for squirming on the adjoining pillow and glaring off at the dim, hand-decorated wall? When does the taste of watercress grow tiresome and unsavory, almost bitter, and the aroma of gingerbread and custard cloy? When, more darkly, does the ugly worm of shame appear, at being linked in the world's esteem (I, a shipwrecked cosmopolitan) with a remote-shore Mother Gooser, whose ceaseless industry produces crowds of oddball clocks that don't tell time, squads of grinning, blue-faced boyboys and gollygirls, boxes' and boxes' worth of squat unstable minichairs and minitables and lumpish giant toads, all festooned preposterously with hand-painted flowers and designs—cosmopolitan me, paired up with someone who transacts for her metier at schlock-shoppes in a tourist village . . . someone sharp as a fresh-milled tack who nevertheless can't spell at all, and counts via her fingers and toes, and keeps accounts with a wedge of old, licked pencil, and reads aloud with a tracing finger and laborious, guffawing effort? Someone who is forever correcting the whole world on the question of her elfin ancestry—someone who never ceases thumping about at home brandishing a mop, or banging in a nail, or boiling up malodorous pots of glue, or rearranging and rewhitewashing and replanting, while someone else would just like to lie around and smooch, or maybe just mope a bit, and muse? . . .

When, precisely, I want to know, do I find myself dreaming undeniably of a normal run of girl . . . a girl who doesn't stay up all night whimpering and massaging her swollen ears when the moon is full; a girl who might actually frisk about in pretty girls' shoes, instead of vigorously polished, bulb-toed clodhoppers; a girl who isn't every other day giving herself a strange new haircut with gardening shears; a girl who doesn't favor ludicrous wobbly flowerpot hats—a girl who might lounge for an afternoon half-naked in the sun on the beach, instead of keeping to the shade in a kind of eccentric, high-buttoned grandma's frock and grandpa's straw hat, with a facial poultice of cucumbers and 'cress spread carefully over her visage? A girl without an insatiable appetite for being constantly read aloud to! A normal, regular girl, without the incessant chirping and buzzing attendance of the bluebird, which one day in a fit of frayed temper I curse as "Pestilent!" and so provoke an answering fit of outrage.

When, when, alas. . . . These are sad questions all; such sad questions. . . . How could it be, I would tax myself, strolling glumly solo along the beach, that I've found the one I love as the silver, shiny apple of my heart of hearts, as she loves me . . . and yet . . . and yet I'm not really happy, honestly, genuinely, at all? . . . How could this be so, for one washed ashore, like me, into an idyll? Oh sad question . . .

And then, besides, there's just the ongoing difficult business of myself (speaking again in all intimacy). Me —that likeable, even charming, citizen, that tenderheart who composes these misty recollections, who nevertheless has been prone to a lifetime of rotten moods, of envies and ambitions, of petulant sulkings and broodings that would drive a cottage-mate to distraction; of torments too indiscreet to mention even here. In other words, a troubled soul, given alas to irrepressible sarcasm, to teasings that finally draw elfin tears, to gnawing, insatiable contempt, even for an idyll. . . . There I go again, on my late afternoon way, slouching along between the waves and the inane motley of vegetation, and then slowing abreast of that certain palm, to scowl forlornly at the upright carcass of my boat, at its fractured keel now adorned with idiotic, hand-painted goodwill totems of industrious, wiggling feet. Real toadstools sprout among the multiple, cartoon-style representations of flapping motion. I curse evilly, and walk out onto the sand, and stare off at the horizon, and think of other places in that way that is fierce and festering, and hardened against loving affection. . . .

The final crisis comes abruptly, with a stunning bluntness that seems the mode life employs for such occasions. My pen trembles and hesitates to record it here. I'll persist, misty-inked, as I can. . . . Briefly, briefly: I go off for a while on a bus trip inland—our very first separation. I come back, unhappy and perversely rancorous (I'd written back exactly one desultory card) and very quickly I receive rancor in reply. She is at the height of annual village-jumble-fair-week hysteria with her toys. I make the truly terrible mistake of clapping up my lovingly decorated, mutually purchased travel bag in a huff, and shouting good-bye and good riddance to one and *all* (kicking a pile of blue stump folk out of my way), and spending the night in the village. When gruffly I try to return a day later, to my astonishment she locks the door against me. When I force my way in, protesting loudly, she wrenches away, and to my shock and horror, from the depths of her pots and brushes and half-assembled heaps of things, she announces—in her blue smock, paint-smudged, her grand ears inflamed from the stage of the moon, her ginger hair cut in stark, grotesque fashion—she announces, wide-eyed, in a strange, fluting voice, that suddenly she understands *everything:* that it can never really work between us! That there and then, irrevocably, it's over—it's *over*! And she flings aside the bag of sweets I'd thrust on her, scattering the contents like stones. It's a truly terrible moment . . . as if she gripped in her hands the musical instrument representing my world (a harp?), and snapped it in half, and tore out the strings. My pen trembles and wavers. . . .

One more horrendous scene lies ahead, at the toy-crowded mantle, involving the great wooden mallet for emergencies, but I can't bring myself to furnish full detail. It's inevitable, of course. It takes place first at the mantle, and then moves to the cottage threshold, as the bluebird screams and goes for my eyes under the trailing bougainvillea, and a horrid, malevolent voice keeps shrieking, "It's over! You've *transgressed*! It's *over*! It's *over*!!" and the wood batters me, driving me back a step at a time, down into the brook and the transplantings of watercress. . . .

I suppose I pretty much lose my mind for a while after this . . . lose my mind from grief and regret and longing, from the simple pain of loss, from a once-beloved's shocking conversion to vengeful savagery. My life enters a quite dreadful era of darkness . . . but I shan't be telling about that here. It's another entire story, you'll have to find it elsewhere. Here I close my eyes to it; and they throb with tears. . . . You see, I just want this to be an account of an idyll . . . of a lost enchantment. I dwell on it to this very day still, though not as ceaselessly as I admit I used to. And I ask myself, why is it that life, or fortune, builds its crooked road with tears, like cobblestones? . . . I'm really not my old cosmopolitan self still yet, but I've been assured that this feebleness that lingers, deep within, will pass away at long last. And yet, more than sometimes, I wonder. . . .

I live alone these days in a small, nondescript rental not far from the village, on the side away from the sea, and its remains. I keep to myself, no doubt more than I should. Semistranded? . . . I think a lot, and ask myself some sad, difficult questions, and try to write, about a number of things. But the work is slow going (mist-hampered). . . . I haven't seen her for more than two years now. It's been best, for me, to avoid her altogether. Perhaps I should really contemplate leaving the goony phantoms of this part of the world for good. . . . Perhaps. . . .

I used to walk into the village every weekend, to a dim sort of place that serves watercress salad to the natives and makes its own desserts on Saturdays. But they knew about me there, about my ruined idyll. "Oh yeah," someone would inevitably mutter, turning heavily toward my corner table from their stool at the counter, "you're that poor shipwrecked guy, who used to go with that fairy gal out by the beach. . . ." But I grew tired of the tremor that would go through me then, and the sound of the alien, quaking, green-and-caramel-flecked voice (my own) pronouncing that long-regretted correction in reply.

9.

Blossom

Blossom

After almost a full hour of it, I get temporarily tired of crying, and I take a break for a while. I push open the screen door and go out a little way onto the back path, and lean against the trunk of a palm. I sigh in long, tremulous, catching breaths and stare out at the other palms exhibiting their ponderous crowns into the evening air. The sea breeze softly gusts, and the sweet mildness sends a fresh stab of pain through me, and I dab at the hot drift on my cheeks. The flesh there feels just like old rubber, so abused and fatigued. "Jesus," I burble to myself, in tearstained apostrophe, rubbing overfamiliarly at my eyes with the back of a hand, "is this how it's going to be for the rest of my life, because of one girl—any lovely moment or thing makes me weep in reminiscence and regret?" As if in answer, my eye is caught by a big, red-tinted blossom nodding on a bush close by—a gorgeous, opulent, benevolent bloom. Immediately I'm reminded of the crimson attraction of her mouth, decorated for an evening out, and my heart's edges buzz with the most delicate and insidious grief. I turn away, starting to sob horribly in earnest, and slump against the jagged, basket-woven trunk, my sobs pulsing up into the cooling, twilight air, my shoulders trembling under the burden of my loss. And so it starts up all over again.

Apparition

I BECOME DISTURBED IN MY INTIMATE MIND, AND WITHDRAW FROM THE SOCIETY OF PEOPLE ALTOgether and live in crude isolation by the sea. I fashion a sort of primitive shelter from driftwood and palm litter on a remote, dismal stretch of beach. I eat the fish I manage laboriously to capture, and coconuts and wild-growing plants. At night the waves rumble all about me, adding their commotion to the state of my being. One day the body of a girl washes up on the sand. The corpse is bloated, its flesh swollen up over the blackened, twisted straps of its bikini. I stare at it. The flesh is plump and slick and greenishly translucent. I go back to my shelter and hurriedly collect the few implements I have scavenged into my possession, and I flee clattering down the beach from this ghastly intrusion.

I pass headland after headland, and the stars come up and wander away. Finally I find a suitable spot to set up another little encampment. At nights, I sit rocking back and forth in the windy darkness, staring out haggardly at the mammoth approach of the waves, at their vast, turbulent, endless chaos of arrival. My soul feels stark and threatened, filled with foreboding. Sometimes, in what must be my dreams, the drowned girl appears in her mossy bikini, to haunt me. She stands swaying in the rude mouth of my shelter. I watch in terror as she enters sluggishly and sinks down at my feet. "What is it you want with me?" I whisper in my horror. "Can't you tell, I just need to be left alone, I cannot be with others now." But I can't find the voice to speak. It comes to me with flickering, dreadful insight that this apparition is come to instruct me, and I force myself to peer grimacing into the dead girl's gruesome, sea-blown face, into the vacant gape of her cloudy, ruined eyes, searching for an oracle of my distress. Behind her, the waves fracture the moonlight as they tumble in slowly in their long, inexorable arrays of chaos.

Relics

My girlfriend dumps me and takes my identity with her when she runs off. After several days of inert shock and outrage I reassemble my wits enough to set out after her. But very quickly the trail goes cold. By the end of a couple of weeks of pathetic meandering, I've lost all track, all hope, of her.

I find myself out in remote territory, in a rooming house in a settlement on the edge of a vast excavation. All day the wind blows dust and branches of weed across the dirt main thoroughfare. I lie on my bunk, null and desolated, listening for hours to the gusts of the wind, watching the pale light moving across the grimy wall above the toes of my boots. Eventually I rise and go heavily across to the open suitcase, and pull out the blouse with little prints of apples all over it—a blouse just like the one that belonged to her. I force my arms through the sleeves, though they're many sizes too small. I prop on my head the wig from the suitcase, and in this ludicrous and disturbing paraphernalia, I lean over the washbowl and stare into the scrap of mirror hung from its nail. Sometimes the entirety of an hour will go by as I strain haplessly for a sense of connection and recognition—a shard of authenticity. "Whose unfeatured face can this be?" I moan wanly, fumbling at my sad, unloved, unshaven cheeks. "Where is its history? What is its fate? Why should it nurture any hope at all?" I turn away, suddenly beside myself. "What has she done to me?" I splutter, and I seize the synthetic reminiscent locks from my head and spit into them and hurl them with all my desiccated might against the wall. I flounder this way and that, in a frenzy of raging. Then I press my blank face into my hands and burst into tears, and lurching over I scramble for the wig at the foot of the wall, and sink onto my bunk with it, clutching it to my apple-strewn breast. I weep in utter, silent, abject abandonment, tossing my eroded head from side to side. The wind beleaguers the windowpane, echoing the insistence of my madness.

Every accumulation of days, I force myself to make my way out of doors. The landlady watches me through thick, prying spectacles. Beside her on the table lies the register, where a forlorn patchwork of crossings out darkens the line where my signature should be. For this irregularity she adds an additional tariff and a constant scowl of contempt and suspicion. I plod doggedly past her into the wind, out into the shabby simulation of a main street, on out into the raw countryside beyond.

The excavation site is an enormous cavity in the pulp of the tormented earth. I squat down close to the edge of the rim, my hand mooring the wig in place against the avaricious gusts. Below me the spectacle gapes in its immensity, on a scale out of a mythic, overwhelming past. Figures of barely clothed men, tiny and dust-caked in the distances, swarm over the exposed slopes, dragging loose enormous, ugly segments of archeological relics. Massive, rudely constructed devices of leverage haul the relics to vast piled storages, there to await classification, presumably, and shipment. What exactly the great bits and pieces that are being quarried signify, from what gigantic, long-lost culture they originate, I never divine. I remain a dumb, loonily accoutred onlooker, squinting through the blowing dust at the epic spectacle of milling and drudgery, of swarming, and violent unearthing. Occasionally a dispute forms like a clot on the slopes and then erupts into a frenzy. The piecemeal agitation of tiny voices reaches me high on my perch. I blink grimly as a minute naked thing—a speck of meagerness—is carried off eventually through the looming, jumbled piles. I turn away. All about me here on my windblown height lies the inconsequential litter of disturbed, uprooted culture. Slivers and fragments of shards are everywhere, trampled and scattered by the colossal exploits below. I run my finger over a little stony something—a nose? an ear? a spoon? I muse distractedly on this crumb of metaphor, my soul clogged with its sludge of misery, as the unceasing wind blows in my ears, blows the dust into my agitated, flapping thatch of curls, into the upturned schoolgirl collar of my apple-spattered blouse.

When the sun scrapes the opposing rim, I rise to my feet and start my tramp back. My poverty of life, my shrunken, anonymous hopelessness, renew their unending grip on me. With each slow step I peer from bleak habit this way and that, over the wind-scoured stubble, for any marks that might suggest her passage or remind me of her presence, of who it is I really am.

THE VISIT

I WAKE UP IN THE MIDDLE OF THE NIGHT. MY EX-BELOVED IS IN THE ROOM WITH ME. MY HEART throbs in shock. "My God, what are you doing here?" I blurt groggily in a sleep-dampened voice. She regards me impassively from the armchair, like a charmingly grave pupil. "It's nothing," she says, shrugging. "It doesn't mean anything. I'm just visiting for a few minutes." I stare through the moonlight dimness at her. She's wearing her heavy cotton blouse with the big, now-faded stripes. We bought it together. Her hair is unkempt, she doesn't wear any lipstick, her head looks small. She looks so very young. Tears start trickling down my cheeks. My eyes throb with them. I restrain myself from asking how she is. She watches me stonily, like an intransigent child. "You shouldn't have come like this," I whisper, my voice creaking. "It's not fair, it does no good." "I know. But it doesn't mean anything," she insists flatly. "It's just . . . sometimes . . ." Her voice trails into silence. The moonlight casts a feeble, pale grid on one side of her face, onto the charming, boyish brush of her hair. I hear her sniffing. My heart breaks. "Why do you have to hurt us both like you do?" I blurt out hopelessly from the depths of my wound. "Why won't you ever let us try again, why must you do this to us—why, why?" There's silence. She sniffs. "You know the answer," she murmurs. Her tone is implacable, matter-of-fact. I shake my head slowly, miserably. "I still can't believe you're saying these things to me," I tell her. "But why shouldn't I be?" she replies, on a note of placid surprise. I turn away, shaking my head. I run my hand the length of my face. It's completely wet. The pillow is soaking wet to my cheek. "You shouldn't have come," I whisper again bitterly. "I'm sorry, I shouldn't have come," she says, her voice falling across mine from behind me. "Go to sleep. Just think of it as an unpleasant dream you've been having. . . ." I rub a knuckle back and forth across the wallpaper. The room over my shoulder is full of deep silence and moonlight. I don't turn around again. I don't hear the door close before I drift back down into sleep.

Night Thoughts

I REACH THE SAD OPINION THAT I HAVE BEEN IRREPARABLY DAMAGED FOR THE REST OF MY LIFE BY A BROken heart. I'm diminished and enfeebled, subtly but essentially. I have a flaw now in the quick of my soul, a wound that will never quite heal, will never quite be as good as new. I believe my capacity for joy has been permanently disabled. I say "joy" as opposed to "happiness," because I mean something profoundly basic—the sense, I suppose, that life fundamentally works out for the good, that the great connection that was lost from childhood might be reclaimed, in new forms of trust, with a beloved companion. It's this harmonizing, this affinity, this sharing of the soul's secret speech that I mean.

And what has happened to me in my heartbreak is such a calamity, to me, it's really beyond consoling. You see, I met her, the heart of my heart, and for a while we were together, but we parted. And I just don't think I shall ever get over it, and be whole again, and get on.

Toy

I have a toy that I keep, that hurts me. It's a sort of fetish object, a kind of doll. A big wooden rose is what it is, crudely fabricated by the hand of my imagination, set on a thorny stem, and painted in the image of one I loved. There I've rendered her wide-set gray eyes, her broad, lovely cheeks, her eccentric thatch of hair, which is now a grandiose ruff of dark blue rose petals.

I've animated this artifact with my memories, my longings, my sadness. True to life, my keepsake savages me as I lie with my head beside it on the pillow, it hisses at me wrathfully as I try to stroke it, and furiously sticks its thorns in when I hold it to my cheek. My friends think I'm out of my mind. "Will you look at yourself in the mirror?" they protest. "Do you want to lose an eye one of these days? Do you want scars for life? What possible reward can there be at this cost?" They throw up their hands. "Please—for want of a better term, grow up," they insist. "Put it away, *throw* it away, it's unhealthy for a guy your age to be transfixed by a malignant knickknack!"

But I can't relinquish it. I laugh sheepishly at my predicament. "But it's so sweet," I tell them. "I just love it so. It's an emotional memento, you see. You know how love can get. . . . It reminds me . . . of things. . . ." At night, I lie in the dark, tenderly whispering to it through tears. "There, there," I try to reassure it, "I understand, I understand. . . ." I shut my eyes against the pain as my pretty toy rages in my scarified embrace, as it tears at me with its dark, jagged thorns, gouging me with its hard, sharp, lovable petals.

Poetry

My girlfriend leaves me. I become so unhinged that I douse myself with flammable liquid and set myself on fire. I squat in an awkward, hideous position on the sidewalk, bleating her name as I gasp in shock at what I've done. The chaos of flames envelopes me, and the air about me trembles. Passersby scramble away into the street in horror, their faces covered behind their arms. Their screaming gives way to the shrieking of sirens. I topple stiffly onto my side, crackling, unconscious.

I awaken in a hospital. Gradually I grow aware of myself as a load of numbness, suspended over an abyss of pain. I perceive glimpses of the pain in the form of twinges that are shocking in their intimation of whence they arise—like the icy wisps that drift in from the fringes of a gigantic, appalling storm. I realize I have transformed myself into a gross, carbonized scrap of the natural world. I lie immobile in my sarcophagus of gauze in the dim light of drawn blinds. With my one uncovered eye I fix on the cloudy gaze of the plastic bottle above my bed. A garish red hose carries the turbid milk from this vessel down to me. This is now my vital nourishment: a semitranslucent, syrupy liquid that suppresses a pain that would annihilate every tissue of my being. My eye blinks, and behind it quavers a thought in commentary: Yes, how appropriate . . . how very sad and appropriate. . . .

Periodically a doctor enters my room. He peers

down at me. He is youngish, balding, a realist of a certain type. "So, you've done it," he declares quietly, brisk and wry. He glances over my little prosthetic world. "You've turned the emotional into the physical. You're a *poet. . . .*" He shakes his head at my chart and raises his eyebrows with a sigh. "It's all about a girl," he proclaims feelingly. "It's all about a wonderful girl!"

Under my bandages, a thrill of emotion ripples through me, at his instinctive comprehension. Through charred, unguent-shiny lips, I whisper to him the half-sacred syllables of her name. "Don't try to answer," he comments, examining his watch. "No point in it, you're nowhere near capable of speech yet." He looks up and grins. "Know how I know it's a girl?" he asks waggishly. He displays his clipboard. "Because it says here you soaked yourself in cognac," he announces. "It's always a girl when it's cognac instead of gasoline!" He pulls an appreciative face. "And the expensive stuff too," he adds, "going by the bottle they found. My, my, such a waste." He gives a little wink. He heads for the door. "Ah, you poets!" he cries, flinging aloft a sardonic hand. "What did you light it with, a dried rose?"

Dust

I FEEL SO BAD AFTER MY GIRLFRIEND DUMPS ME THAT FINALLY I PUT A ROPE AROUND MY NECK, AND END IT all. After a few minutes' terrible struggle I hang from the ceiling. A night passes and most of a day. They find me. They cut me down and fumble with my tongue and telephone the morgue. But then something or other distracts them, and I'm left alone.

I sit up. I feel ill and very, very strange, and mortally ashamed of what I've done, once people find out. I get heavily to my feet by means of the upturned chair, and stumble out across the open threshold of the apartment, thudding against the doorjamb, and go lurching off into the evening darkness.

The rest of the night, and the following day and night, are a blurred smear, mainly of alleyways. At last I drift out to the outskirts of town, and then down to the banks of the river. It's a dismal, trash-strewn acreage, under an abandoned railroad trestle. Others like myself are huddled there, bearing the marks of their shame. They scowl over at me dolorously. I slump on the dusty earth away from them, tugging up my soiled jacket collar over the remains of my lethal necklace and its fibrous stump. I rock back and forth, arms clasped about myself, staring numbly at the discolored water, at its queasy, littered rim at the foot of the bank. I turn my head and look forlornly toward the others. They stare back at me. "Oh dearest God, what have I wrought?" I think blankly, turning away. At night, from its abyss, the most abject and appalling noises of weeping sound around me.

A hand jars me awake. It's morning. To my shock my former girlfriend is standing over me. She brandishes something in my face—a newspaper. "What do you think you are doing?" she demands of me. "Tell me! What do you think you are doing?" "Darling . . ." I mumble. The old disabling yearning immediately goes through me at her presence, and the old horror, at her ludicrous, domineering wrathfulness. I try to sit up. The newspaper rattles punitively against my ear. "Do you know what's in here?" she continues. *"Do you?"* I shake my head. I close my eyes for a moment against her familiar, outrageous hectoring. I open them and squint up at her, helplessly adoring. She has on one of those outfits only she could wear: porkpie hat pasted with felt daisies, knee-length denim cutoffs, faded blue calf-length men's socks. She looks like an impoverished, adorable Salvation Army trainee on a fishing weekend. Her bicycle is parked behind her, with picnic basket displaying juts of baguettes above the handlebars. The fond thought stabs me, that she goes on more picnics than anyone I have ever known, with suicide notes: she is shouting about suicide notes—my suicide note. "And it's all about *me*!" she cries, almost bleating. "It has *my name* in it! In the paper! In the *newspaper*!" I feel a sickened shrill of horror. "I'm sorry," I stammer. My voice quavers. "I forgot all about it. I know how sensitive you are about privacy. I'm sorry!" I protest. "Please, forgive me! Forgive me!" "That's all you ever say," she bellows. "It's not good enough! Didn't you ever think how it would make me look? You never *think*!" she cries. And she raises one of her comically oversized but smartly maintained hiking boots and stamps it on the ground. This gesture of pique undoes me. I stare off into the dust, shaking uncontrollably through my limbs. "I can't believe it," I whimper. "Even when I'm driven to killing myself, even here in the company of the dead and the self-destroyed, you still show up and find a way to blame me, and scream at me, and torment me! I can't believe it!" I moan, trembling. "Oh stop it, *stop* it!" she mutters. She casts the newspaper away and walks off, stalking in a big circle, punching her denimed thigh with the heel of a fist. There's ragged silence. I hang my head, my chin sunk on the rope remains, my chest heaving, my breath coming like that of a small heat-stricken dog.

She comes back over and squats beside me and scowls down at me. She puts a hand on my shoulder and gives it a brief impersonal squeeze. I grunt and make a motion of moving from her. She sighs. She looks off. "What unpleasant people," she mutters. She gazes all about, frowning. "What a sickening place!" she adds. I blink grimly. "How did you find me here?" I murmur. She shrugs. "A friend suggested it," she replies. The locution, "a friend," sets off a flame of anguish in me. "Which friend?" I ask thickly. "Someone I know? Someone . . . new?" "Never *mind,*" she replies fiercely. She surveys me with animated displeasure. "You look *awful,*" she announces. "Jesus, thank you, darling," I mutter. She leans close, grimacing. She sniffs. "Your breath smells exactly like *shit*!" she exclaims. "Oh for Christ's sake—" I protest, twisting away. "And why are you still wearing that ridiculous rope?" she demands. She reaches in with powerful, digging fingers. "Ow, stop it—you're *hurting* me!" I cry. I push her away. She gazes at me grimly, in silence. Then she starts to sneer at a new thought. "I suppose you've told them all about me," she declares, waving a hand at the scene behind us. One of her eyelids twitches dangerously. "No, darling, *no,* for God's sake," I moan in alarm. "I promise you, I haven't said a single—" "So what are your plans?" she demands, her tone flaring again. "Answer me: what exactly are you planning to do?" "Darling, I don't *know,*" I protest, whimpering once more under the harshness of her manner. "I only got here last night!" "That's all you ever say!" she cries back. "You don't know—you never know *anything*!"

Suddenly she swarms to her feet. "This is *insane*!" she wails. She claps the back of a hand to her forehead in an astoundingly histrionic gesture, like a deranged troll or tabby cat auditioning for grand opera. She twists this way and that. Her outfit gives the whole display a bizarre, almost frightening tinge. "This is *insane*!" she screams. "Go *away*! Leave me *alone*! Go and *bury* yourself! *Go! Go!*" she roars. I gape up at her, cringing. She stamps again and again on the ground with her boot, in a fury. She clutches her hatted head in a show of writhing. "Darling—please—don't be like this—" I splutter. All at once, she straightens. "I've got to go, I'm going to be late," she declares hectically. She wheels and starts to march off. "No, darling, wait—" I call out, helpless. "Wait! Please, don't—" She spins around. She flings her hands out wide toward me in an immense, biblical gesture. "Can't you think of anyone but *yourself*?" she shrieks. "Just *leave me alone*! Stop *torturing* me!" I sink back down, aghast. In a splintered daze I watch her climb onto her bicycle and reset the checkered cloth of basket and baguettes and launch off bouncing her way through the shadows of the railroad trestle, into the distance.

I turn back panting toward the river. I gape at it, my eyes, my body, throbbing feebly. I heave around again; but there's only the trail of her dust in the air. My gaze drifts toward my neighbors. They stare back, huddled, inert. I whisper something in barely audible horror, and slump over heavily openmouthed into the ground, in a state of despair beyond despair. The rope fibers choke me, until I rearrange them with trembling fingers. Later, a derelict figure squats beside me. He peers down at me. I hear him grunting. A smell of filth assails me. There are horrible messes at the ends of his shirtsleeves. "Oh, brother," he croaks tremulously, shaking his head. "If she was the reason, oh, *brother* . . ." And he makes the squalid little gesture of the lost and defeated, before he moves away.

In Memoriam

I WORK AT MY TABLE, IN HO-HUM FASHION. A NOISE INTRUDES UPON ME: THE SLOW TOLLING OF A BELL. I hearken, puzzled. "But there aren't any churches around here," I think. I put down my pen and go over to the window. Shocked, I throw it open. I stick my head out into the street. The entire thoroughfare has been draped with limp, flowing yards of black crepe. A black-shrouded cortege makes its way along before a grim, grieving crowd. Many carry bloodred roses. The open coffin comes somberly borne along, right under my very window. I gape down at the grisly, poignant figure with its own rose at its dowdy chest. I stare at the sunken-mouthed, cement-hued visage. I gasp, clutching at the window frame. "But my God—that's *me,*" I blurt out, in a stricken voice. "That's me in there, I'd recognize that face anywhere!" I wrench away from the window, knocking my head in the process. Hysterically I feel at my chest, at my pounding heart. I lunge back. But there's no denying it. "That's *me* down there!" I cry out. I come back into the room, gripping my head in my hands. "But how unspeakably horrible!" I think. "And how *alienated,*" I reflect further. "To be an onlooker at one's own funeral! . . ." I grab up my jacket from my chair, and hurry out the door.

From my front steps I press down incognito into the slow-moving, snuffling throng. I've donned my sunglasses, and I turn up my jacket collar. The coffin passes out of sight ahead around the corner. Sinking even deeper below my collar's rim, I tug furtively at the sleeve of a tough-looking old gent slouching along beside me. "Who is it that they're burying, Pop?" I query him out of the side of my mouth. "What happened to him? How did—did he—how did he—die?" The old fellow turns on me a pair of red-rimmed, sluggish eyes. He scowls at me blearily over his sumptuous rose. He doesn't answer. I regard him in confusion. "Excuse me," I stammer. "I don't mean to intrude—I was just wondering—" "Women," he croaks, bitterly. "Women killed him! All the little ways women can hurt a guy, day in, day out. That's what did it. Finally it was too much. It killed him!"

I turn away from this terrible oracle. My steps falter and a sob stabs through my heart. Tears flood my eyes. "Of course!" I think, clutching a hand to my cheek. "Now I understand everything—the roses and what have you. This is all some sort of inner spectacle, conjured up by my deepest psyche, to represent what women have done to me. Yes, it's absolutely true, they've killed me!" I reflect, embracing this intimate apocalypse. The experiences of the last numerous months come swarming back: it's all been too much, all those awful, vicious girls with their false promises, their broken appointments and unreturned phone calls, their enticing conversations that imply every prospect of intimacy and really only prefigure disappointment and disdain, and despair. "All of that, on top of years of a broken heart," I cry out internally, "and it's finally undone me. It's *killed* me!"

My legs turn infirm under the knell of this last, piercingly lugubrious sentence. The scene swims about me in the greenish purple of my sunglasses. I surrender myself to the drift of mourners, more or less to be carried along.

We enter a discreet graveyard. My heart is ravaged

now with full childlike sorrow for myself, and enough maneuvering room clears for me to fall to my knees on the turf somewhere near graveside. I weep among the antique headstones as a minister's voice intones over the sealing and lowering of the coffin, over its thumping adieus of roses, its final soil-covering from the hazards of the world and its women. The faint tones of a distant bell drift overhead. I become aware that my grief is actually among the most prominent of those in attendance, and I feel a twinge of self-consciousness at this, in conjunction with the fact that my sunglasses, I realize, are of the tropical-beach-wear variety. But then I think, why bloody not, it's altogether appropriate I should grieve in whatever manner I please, as much as I want, given my relationship to the one being interred! Freely I sob away.

The service ends. I climb to my feet, groggy and numbed by emotion. I feel a tremendous, tender solicitude for my departed self-representation and its troubles with the other half of the species, and a deeply personal, narcissistic pride at the heartrending splendors of commemoration fabricated by my psyche in its metaphorizing labors. I turn to take my leave. After a few steps, I slowly halt. A figure off to the side is packing up a tripod. The official photographer . . . he's been photographing the proceedings. An enormous inspiration blooms inside me, as I regard him, like the sum of all the roses piled on my coffin. There will be documents of all of this. What is to stop me from ordering up large-scale copies of particularly funereal images and shipping them to every last female responsible, to acquaint them, to their everlasting guilt and shame, with what they have wrought?

I hurry on over. The photographer is worrying now at a lever on his camera. He looks up at me unwarmly.

"Are you a member of the family?" he mutters, after hearing my request. "*What?* Well, no—not exactly," I reply, taken aback. A mixture of agitation, and embarrassment at the peculiar nature of the circumstances, confounds me. "I mean," I tell him, "I'm actually—I mean, don't you—" My face turns bright red. "I mean, for God's sake, don't you recognize me?" I blurt out. I remember the sunglasses and I snatch them off. I thrust my face up out from my collar. The photographer leans away, frowning perplexedly. He shakes his head from side to side. "For Christ's sake, you can't tell? It's me, it's me in there!" I sputter vehemently, gesturing wildly toward the grave. "I'm the guy they just buried—I mean, a *version* of me, a psychological replica! Can't you *see*?" The photographer claps his head. "Of course, of course!" he cries. "Now I—jeez, I'm so sorry, I'm such a blind idiot, I go to so many of these. . . ." My legs are trembling. "So you'll send me copies," I murmur in a strained voice. "Well of course, of course I will," he says. "Soon as I get clear of a couple from last week. Say, listen, do please forgive me, I know how—" I swing away, overcome abruptly by all the screwy, harrowing intensities of the past hour, by the blatant neuroticness of the whole situation. "I'm *really* sorry—" he calls after me, as I lurch away. "It's all right—" I mumble. I wave a hand clumsily behind me.

I feel my composure disintegrating in almost palpable shreds, and I struggle just not to crumple into jibbering segments. The late stragglers part for me as I come weaving through the headstones in my lurid eyepieces. I can hear them pointing me out. The preposterous vainglory of my psycho-spectacle now engulfs me with the force of a shocking nakedness. I veer along half stumbling in a cringing daze, fists pressed rigidly into my pockets, the tears streaming down from under my lenses. "The poor, wretched man, there he is," I can hear them murmuring and clucking as I pass. "Destroyed by women . . . by women, utterly destroyed!"

Interrogation

There's a loud thudding at my door. It's the police. They take me down to a squat, drab building. I'm led into a shadowy room. A figure stands half-hidden behind the glare of a work lamp turned spotlight fashion. A photograph is thrust at me. "Who is this person?" the obscured man demands. I squint at the face caught by the camera. Slowly I raise my head, shielding my eyes with my hand against the light. "Why, it's me," I answer, confused. "Then why do you look like that?" the demand comes bluntly. "I'm not sure I know exactly—what you mean—" I stammer, although it's obvious as the nose on my face how I look: I look as if the weight of the world had been condensed into a kind of gel and smeared across my brow. "You know what I mean," the man says quietly. "Quit stalling!" he cries. "Why are you, for all intents and purposes, *impersonating a corpse*?" I swallow. I grimace in the overbrilliant light. "I'm afraid I really don't . . ." I begin evasively, but my voice trails off. Suddenly a sap of desperate anger swells in me. "Listen, am I under arrest or what?" I hear myself protest. "Because if I am, I believe I'm entitled to a lawyer, and I believe—" But I don't know what to say next. There's silence. My hands are trembling. Cigarette smoke curls very slowly down into the blazing light. Suddenly there's a snap, and pitch blackness. The room blooms into soft, indirect illumination. A tall, rugged guy comes around the desk. He looks like a fit, old-fashioned campaigner with the iron gray bristles of his crewcut. "Nah, you're not under arrest," he says calmly. He lifts a heavy arm and surrounds my shoulders with it and presses with a muscular compassion. A deep twinge of emotion resounds through me, and my breath falters. I have to fight to hold back tears. My head is bowed. The guy jostles me tenderly as he leads me slowly toward the door. "Hey, that's okay, that's okay," he murmurs. His breath smells of cigarettes. "We understand—believe me, we sympathize. We know what love can do," he says. "But you just can't go around simulating a carcass!" The reasonableness of his tone is tinged with the heft of authority. He takes his arm down. "We just can't have people loose out there acting like they were dead," he appeals to me. "It causes problems, for everybody. And we have *enough* problems. Don't we?" he says. I nod, standing in the doorway. My eyes are fixed on the floor as I try to master my emotions. There's a long moment of silence. The guy surveys me. Then he shifts his gaze, and signals to someone behind me. "So you think about it?" he says. I nod again. A gloved hand takes charge of my elbow, and the door closes shut, as I turn to follow, to be discharged.

ABOVE THE ROOFS

I GO TO BED. THE GOLDEN MOON HAS RISEN SLOWLY INTO THE NIGHT SKY AND HANGS OVER THE ROOFS OF the sleeping town. It drifts along humdrum among the stars until it's framed between the curtains of my window. It peers down from its height. In my sleep I flinch slightly as the golden vapor of moonlight floats into the shadows of my room and bed. The moon observes me. On an impulse, out of tedium, it amuses itself by transforming the features of its big face into those of my former beloved. It sets its eyes wide and colors them blue-gray, and rouges its mouth and lightly dusts its upper lip with down, and grows a thatch of hazel hair cut in eccentric schoolboy fashion. Mischievously it fits on its head that jaunty, birthday-present cricket cap, dark green with a yellow circle drawn in it. In my bed, a quiver of pain and longing jars my sleep. "Darling!—" I call out, twisting on my pillow. My hands fumble toward the moon. The moon sports a round-collared shirt with a design of tiny fruits for good measure. It puts its big, lovely cheeks in its hands and wrily watches me, amused and absorbed. Tears dampen my cheeks. "Oh please, won't you forgive me?" I whisper in despair. I writhe in the sheets. "Won't you come back?" I implore, my pajama-clad arms floundering in the moonlight, straining every sinew for the beloved visage high in the heavens, up above the dark roofs. The moon turns its head askance in its fingers, grinning, and lets out a little laugh, of embarrassment almost, and amazement, at the havoc its diversion has created.

So the night passes. Slowly my pleading voice grows feeble, and subsides into tearful whimperings and gulps, and, finally again, sleep.

The moon yawns. Around it the night sky grows pale, depleted and exhausted. The moon smiles sleepily to itself and shakes its head at the dolorous, slumbering figure on view through my curtains. It yawns another time, and sighs, and removes its cap, and reassembles its age-old implacable features, now silvered in the dawn. And it sets off across the horizon, to resume its round among the fleeting stars.

Practical Joke

As a practical joke, my girlfriend leaves me. I am utterly heartbroken. Insidiously, it's springtime.

"Oh, come now, it's not all *that* bad," she grins, as we oppose each other al fresco over a café table and its tumbler of blossoms. I have finally managed to arrange a meeting. "Please, won't you come back, darling?" I beseech, my voice quavering plaintively as I lean in. "I do miss you so!" "Oh, you never know, I *might,*" she offers airily, pulling her hand away as she feels mine closing on it. She drops a little wink. "No, darling, *please,*" I insist, twisting in my chair. "This is madness! Enough is enough. I mean, I don't mind a bit of trickery and nasty humor, but this is going too far. You're torturing me!" I protest. "My, how you do love to exaggerate, don't you?" she quips, bringing out a silver case.

I watch in anguished affection as she replenishes the rouge on her lips, as the big sun warms us with its long-awaited regard. I can hear a noise I make involuntarily, like a puppy's whimper. My heart flops wanly in my vitals. *"Please? . . ."* I whisper, in agony. My girlfriend lets out a hooting laugh and claps her compact up. "Now, you're never going to get me back with *that,*" she admonishes jauntily. She signals for the waiter. "Oh, we'll just have to see, won't we?" she replies with a secretive smile, when I ask when we can meet again.

I stand by the little check-clothed table and watch

her make her way down the avenue along the richly blooming trees. At the corner, she turns and waves to me, before disappearing. Tears erupt in my eyes. I cry out under my breath. The fragrant breeze pulses over me like a wounding, incomprehensible sadness in the spring sunlight, in the flowering, maniacal season.

THE FIRE

I GO OUT INTO THE GARDEN. SOMEONE IS IN THE WOODS NEARBY, SETTING FIRE TO THE TREES. I shout at them to stop. Smoke billows up and rolls in over the garden fence like a dirty, tumbling, just-woken behemoth. Orange flames sway and quiver and soar. I shout until my voice goes hoarse, but my protests are drowned by the roaring crackle of burning branches and the crashing fall of a fiery weight of treetop. I clamber frantically with a bucket among the green rows of my garden. Suddenly a great, flaming bough comes toppling down across my fence. It sprawls full length among the stakes and fat-bunched leaves, like a skeletal leviathan burning in terrible sacrifice. I rush at it with my bucket, but the searing heat drives me back. Overhead there is a terrific crack. I scream and drop the bucket and dash away through the carefully tilled soil. I take cover behind the potting shed and crouch against its still-cool, whitewashed wall, punching with my fist, weeping in disbelief.

The next day the fire has burned itself out. The woods after all weren't very big. All that's left of them are charred stumps, a broken choral architecture of gray and black. The garden is desolated, acrid smelling. Beside each other in the scorched, blackened wounds of their impact lie the ruins of two huge branches. The little plump flourishes of green stuff are now just bits of carbonous refuse here and there around them. The sight overwhelms me and I sink down onto a knee in my despair.

Eventually I compose myself. I get the ax and the spade from the damaged potting shed, and begin stolidly to work. A group of figures make their way beyond the charred webbing of the fence. I stop and watch them. They've caught the person who started the fire. They're leading her off somewhere. I know her, I know her peculiar, unhappy history, to which I myself contributed, thoughtlessly and fatefully. I know I should really only pity her. But as the group comes abreast, I find myself trembling. "Why did you have to do this?" I suddenly shout at her. "Why? Why did you have to cause such terrible devastation?" My voice cracks. The cords of my neck stand out. I grip the handle of the spade with all my quaking rage. But the girl only turns her smoke-scorched, raggedly cropped head mildly to me from among the big, hemming shoulders, and laughs softly with startled embarrassment, childlike and uncomprehending.

10.

Blue

Blue

In the grisly aftertangle of our relationship, I at last summon the personal strength to break off all communication whatsoever with my former beloved, who dumped me. Almost immediately, this vacuum grows infested with outrage. The insidious, the monstrous, the truly and preposterously vile abuses I allowed myself to suffer in the abject hopes of reconciliation now swarm back to mind, clawing at me, gnawing at me, squealing their rancid memories in my face. For days on end I writhe behind drawn shades. Horrible, venomous epithets deform lips that used to coo. Fists that once brought flowers now lash continuously at the stale air, while I heave about screeching my grievances at the walls, howling for justice and revenge. But to what avail? Showy acts of bodily assault are just not my style, for various reasons, including (to my shame and consternation) a dreadful, morbid, lingering tenderness—despite everything—for my outlandish tormentor.

Madness begins to hear its cue, and rolls its shoulders in the wings.

And then just like that, one hoarse, haggard afternoon, as if in a vision a stroke of genius presents the solution. It's simple, it's awe-inspiring. And it won't actually harm a soul. It's my imagination! "What is to stop me," I ask myself, "from mentally constructing the figment of that endearing but *egregious thorn* of my heart, and subjecting this incarnation of her to the full extent of vengeful what-for she so justly has coming?" A little cackle rises in my throat, like a loose screw. "Why, nothing," I whisper, trembling, through the fingers clamped against my mouth. "Why, absolutely nothing! . . ." I try to sit back down to calm myself, but I can't.

The first session of make-believe almost right away gets out of hand. In my daydream vigilantism, I haul her doppelgänger out of a nap by the scruff of her neck and subject her right there and then kicking and squalling to a vicious public spanking, with her own tortoiseshell hairbrush, in recompense for certain grotesquely spiteful misdeeds of a social—sexual—nature. I work up into such a frenzy the hairbrush goes right through her exposed, pale bottom. I leave off chaotically, and have her carted down on the spur of the moment to an ad-hoc dunking stool rigged up over a hastily improvised village pond, and as she plunges and reemerges, choking and thrashing, I stalk about the bank ranting at her at the top of my voice, flailing my fists spastically everywhere, the strings and gobs of drool swinging out from my nose and lips.

The next morning, finally stirring, I'm shaken and somber. I sip gooey tea with honey and lemon for my throat, swollen and shattered from the torrents of autothespianisms, and shift about uncomfortably as the subtitle *Goes Berserk!* blinks over and over across certain portions of internal news footage. My head sinks toward my shoulders. I admonish myself, that even under extraordinary emotional duress, even within the most private inner sanctums of my mind, there remain standards of composure, of basic humanity and decency. "After all," I remind myself, "the whole purpose of this inventive, possibly bizarre, program is for the sake of my emotional health, to provide means to redress—not commit—certain disgraceful emotional misbehaviors. Certain utterly outrageous, probably *criminal* emotional wrongdoings . . ." I add. I hear my teeth grinding. My throat starts to ache again. Suddenly I whack myself on the thigh with my hand. "Hey come *on,*" I exhort out loud, my voice wincingly below hearing. "Where's that puckish touch I'm so famous for? Where's the whimsy? Let's not forget our sense of humor in all this, shall we?" I adjure.

After more tea, and a good long, scheming shower, I go about surprising my simulated quarry, at tea herself. As she leaps from her chair in protest, I flip a flippant wave of fingers, and transform her just like that into a creature I used to tease her with resembling, in more affectionate days—to wit, a garden mole. Off she darts among the furniture, all apanic, still wearing the pink headband she had on, now scaled down. Delighted, I get hold of a broom and beat it over the armchair she's sought refuge under, and watch her shoot out blindly on her little scurrying legs, off along the baseboard and around into the bedroom. I pull on the gloves I've brought along and saunter in after her, much amused. I corner her after a bit of doing and grab her off the floor behind the futon, and hold her up in both hands for inspection—hairy, wriggling body, petite churning trotters with their nasty, digging nails, teeny pinched snout with its gnashing teeth and sleepy slit eyes under its pink headband. "This is you, alright, in a nutshell," I chuckle, shaking my head at the sight of what's in my grip. "You hairy, spitting, infantile—*rodent*!" For an instant the image seethes, of me turning and hurling her with all, sickening might against the wall, like a diner enraged at the cooking of his bratwurst. But then I swallow, and let out a shaky laugh, and return her, perhaps a little heavily, to the floor. She rights herself frantically and scurries off at desperate speed toward the threshold.

Just as she reaches it, I rewiggle a glove, and with a cartoonish "pfut!" she's transformed again, into a kangaroo—a stuffed, thigh-high, toy-arcade replica of another creature from my private menagerie of her. This one perhaps a bit too cruel for exposure at times previous. *But not now!* Gleefully I regard the orange terrycloth fur, the hefty lower legs and tail, the slight, sloping shoulders, the goofy muzzle with black-olive nose, big bright eyes, huge upstanding ears. "A waltz, my malignant Matilda?" I inquire. With venomous expertise I bestow the exact quantum of animation on her, and then make as if to rush up behind, and off she goes, hopping in the air. I pursue her all around the apartment in a mocking, lumbering cakewalk, roaring with bloodthirsty delight as she thuds along in upright, flatfooted fashion, paws held high, all the while fixing me over her narrow shoulder with typical childish ferocity, her little mouth twisted to one side, her big teeth gritting. I'm having such a grand time I have to slump against a wall just to catch my breath. And then out of nowhere, unbidden, unwelcome, a dark tremor of sadness goes through me; and I gaze with misting eyes at the decorative figments of what I lived among for so many days . . . at the funny old teapot and mugs of hers, on the table she salvaged from the street . . . at the paint-by-numbers icon of a house in the woods that would greet me every morning on my way into the narrow kitchen to make our coffee. A painful bubble swells in my throat.

I have to remove myself back to my shade-drawn living room, where I pace about thumping both fists against both thighs, sniffing and gulping, my cheeks glistening, while I curse my betraying heart, my heart in its tumult. . . .

I realize I have to be far more wary and cautious with the procedure I've initiated. The passions, the painful intensities involved, are fearsome, wrenching, as volatile in their way as badly packed chemicals. "A wounded, angry heart, as the world knows," I observe, "is an errant hodgepodge of poignantly explosive contradictions." And I'm mindful too that my general psychological apparatus, considered overall, is not exactly a model of stability these days, what with the traumatic stresses of my recent affairs. "What's required now, above all else," I counsel myself, "is method and discipline. I need clear objectives, and, how should I say, an almost detached, well-nigh *scientific* strategy toward those ends. I cannot," I admonish, beleaguering my leg eternally for emphasis, "be like some"—I forage for *le mot juste*—"some *seal pup*, sloshing about wherever the tides of his impulse take him. In those waters," I muse grimly, "I could easily drown. . . ."

I decide to draw up a list, on a clean sheet of paper, of the exact priority of grievances to be addressed. From this I will derive my design specifications, so to speak. I clear my table of rubble, and set to work. Not unexpectedly, a certain phrase and its kin appear at the top, in block letters. All variants of her beloved penchant, in our late days of chaos, for insufferable, galling, yammering *bombast*! I doodle in the margin beside the entries, scowling, musing on windbag pegs being dragged down from high horses. I start to make holes in the paper. My mind twitches this way, then—Suddenly I curse at what I'm back doing. I snatch up my hand to hurl the ballpoint at the carpet; but then I just don't. Very deliberately, I replace the pen on the table. I sit, taking long, trembling breaths, laboring to apply my tumultuous self in the spirit of pseudoscientific creative rigor.

I manage to formulate an inner scenario, on the theme of sanctimonious pomposity. I construct, in the theatrical lab of my brain, a customized Lower Depths

—a simulated shabby-rooming-house water closet, which I modify to almost the scale of an Augean public-toilet facility. Brooding with ad-hominem precision, I fetch the star of the show on set, and shove her into costume: crude cardboard crown on her head, around her shoulders a laughably homemade flannel robe of state, with "Great Artiste" embroidered on it; in her hand, as scepter of her office and metier, a toilet-bowl brush. I step back inwardly to eye the whole effect. Praise lights up spontaneously in my mind, like a marquee blurb. "Brilliant Tour de Force of Come-Uppance!" it raves. I rub my hands with icy, thrilled determination, and take a deep breath and wish myself a broken leg as I raise the internal curtain.

"Now then, Miss High and Mighty, *Miss Polly Pompous Picasso*!" I commence grandly. "Here's your chance to show off those preeminent talents of yours with a brush, that you were always so fond of blathering on about! You will," I direct, "scrub every one of these several dozen toilet bowls you see aligned before you spick-and-span and shiny clean—every one of which, I hope you'll note," I go on, "brimming with the most splendid blue bowl cleaner, just awaiting your masterly hand! Now what do you think of that?" I inquire. My image of her glares back at me, shamed, subdued. "Go ahead," I coax her. "I've given you power of speech, God knows I wouldn't want you to die from *atrophy of your favorite organ.*" "I think you're awful," she mutters plaintively. "You're so cruel!" "But, my dear . . ." I reply with slowed, triumphant venom, my response well rehearsed for its cue: "Weren't you the very one who informed me, sans invitation, that I *needed* to develop the quote *dark side* unquote of my own teensy, puny, 'superficial' I believe you once characterized it, art—such as the sort of thing we're in the midst of now? So insignificant, *of course,*" I exclaim, "beside *your Grand Pursuit*!!" My voice rasps for one uncontrolled, memory-ravaged moment, but then I'm able to reassert myself. I grin, like a viper with a full set of teeth. I gesture with a courtly flourish at the nearest blue bowl. *"S'il vous plaît,* Your Highness," I declare. "Mind your crown!"

I lounge against the moldy wallpaper, watching with the full gloating steep of vengeful bliss, as my burlesque genius turns slowly and bends to start her labors, snuffling and glowering in her punitive regalia. "And after you've knocked off your first few masterpieces," I add, drawling airily, "as an extrapersonalized dab of sulphur I shall bring in the Polaroid camera you gave me for Christmas, and I'll take some wonderful candid snaps of you right here in your studio, to send to all the newspapers and the art magazines." She wrenches around. "No!" she shouts at me. *"No pictures!"* I regard her, astounded. I push off the wall. "What do you mean, no pictures," I splutter. "That's not your dialogue. How dare you say that? How dare you tell me what I can and cannot do in my own imagination! Get back to your bowl this instant!" To my further shock, she clambers to her feet. She flings down the brush. Blue spatters over the linoleum. "No!" she announces. "There's a limit to the amount of mockery I'll suffer." *"Pick-that-brush-up,"* I snarl, my eyes saucers of rage and disbelief. "I shall not," she replies, folding her arms under her robe and lifting her chin and absurdly crowned head. "Not if you're going to take pictures!" I make a step toward her, fists clenched at my belt. "Do what I say—" I growl lethally through bared, gritted teeth. She cringes. "Oh—*getting physical, are we*?" she cries. I gasp. I falter and twist away from her, gripping my forehead with a maddened hand.

I feel as if a live electric wire had been fed into my chest. I gape off in consternation, mouth hanging wide.

The words she's just spoken repeat exactly the unforgettably starchy melodramatics she annunciated, during one particularly wretched scene from our breakup, when I'd caught hold of her wrist to make her listen. The whole lavatory complex sways around me, as if in a throb of heated air. "But how can this be *happening*?" I whine. How could this figment of my invention be carrying on like this? How could the magnificent construct of my inspired revenge be sent whirling into such shambles? "It's so typical of her," I wail. "For God's sake—*do* something!" I screech out, in desperate confusion, at my supposedly orchestrating self. There's a disorganized pause. "Huh? *Me?* What am *I* supposed to do?" I sputter back, doubly befuddled. Another disjointed pause. Frantically improvising, I posit my inner self to turn and face the regal delinquent, and over a rigid, symbolically menacing finger, in a strangled, deadly voice, inform her that unless she *immediately* cooperates with the scenario as scripted, she will be forced, with all the venomously confidential power I command—*forced*—to repeat over and over and over that lugubrious scene from her traumatically intimate personal history, where, as a pudgy third-grader, she was selected by her classmates as the first person to be eaten, should famine ever force them into cannibalism!

The result is an immediate scream. She stoops, toppling her crown, and snatches up the brush and plunges it into the toilet and whirls. I shout and try to jump clear, but the flying scepter whips a shower of syrupy blue junk across my face and the front of my clothing. I reel back sideways down the wall. I flounder and sputter there, clawing at my face, gasping at the sickeningly aromatic blue all over my hands now, all over my shirt. I lift my head and gape at her, spitting blue into the air. She gapes in return, drawing back, her fury compounded with shock and alarm at what she's done, her hands raised outstretched in self-protection, like a queen astounded in an antique pageant. *"You—you—"* I squawk incoherently. Rage rushes up through me, and galvanizes into a detached force, compressed and ruthless and mad to violate. *"No—"* she cries, as I writhe off the wall and come out a step.

She lurches back in her clownish finery, stumbling against the bowl. I set myself, grimacing at her, hands up beside my head like claws, as if in a parody of the history of mesmerism and telekinesis. *"No!"* she shrieks. She clutches under her nose. A gigantic, luxurious blond handlebar mustache now droops its heavy wings from her once-downy upper lip, over her mouth and out beyond the lines of her jaw. She slumps back against the wall behind the toilet, and sinks slowly toward the blue-stained linoleum, squealing in distress. I sway in place, gasping, half recoiled away from the sight of my terrible handiwork, my appalling hands held like objects in the air, dripping blue gore. The lavatory complex echoes with her slow, wailing sobs, infantlike, her vandalized face wrinkled in complete torment as she fumbles with erratic hands at the hirsute monstrosity now in place. "Why are you so mean to me?" she wails, in almost breathless, agonized quiet. "Why do you always have to hurt me so?"

"Because you hurt me!" I scream, squawking bug-eyed, the mad rancor of the blue in my mouth. "You pompous, vicious, pigheaded tit! *You're just getting what you deserve!!"* She rocks back and forth against the bowl, repeating her question over and over through her grinding sobs, huddled under her emblazoned cloak, the tears rolling down her cheeks into the prodigious depths of her mustache. "And you can just stay there, and contemplate what your pigheaded ways have brought you to!" I shout, feeling delirious, trying to brazen away the horror of what I've done, of her an-

guish. I grab up her cardboard crown from near her feet, clumsily, wildly. "Here," I snarl, "don't forget this, Your High-Falutin' Majes . . ." My voice trails off. I cast the crown aside and stagger a step, and scream.

I lurch about, back in the dingy light of my apartment, howling, clawing at my cheeks as if the flesh were poisoned. I sink sprawling onto the sofa and flounder about there, hugging my gross body in my arms, beside myself. "What have I done?" I squeal. "God, *what have I done*?" I twist this way and that, at one point grappling my arms around my skull, to try to block out the transgressive enormity my wayward imaginings have led to. I chew my wrist, and sob and cry out, and flail my feet against the floor, at my horrors of the heart.

At last, exhausted, I sit slumped, harrowed, just staring ahead. A terrible, wan clarity takes shape now before me. "Yes, that's it," I announce aloud in a flat, cracked whisper. "It's just got to stop. I must simply . . . abandon the whole noble venture lock, stock, and barrel. It's just gone too far! Even though, as always, she's as much to blame—in her own perverse, provocative—but be that as it may, I must now . . . put her out of my mind entirely. I must suspend once and for all *all* contact, even of this most internal variety. I must just *stop:* right here and now. And forever! . . ." I swallow in slow stages, hearing my esophagus laboring. "Yes," I gasp slightly, my eyes blinking wide, my heart chill and portentous and far away. "Before they come to take me to the nuthouse, that is exactly what I must do. . . ."

I keep my word. I encounter her memory only one last time, some months later, in a dream. I am walking through an unfamiliar forest, peering about ruefully under the trees for certain items I have somehow misplaced. All of a sudden she walks right out from behind a rhododendron bush. We stare at each other. She still has the giant mustache. She wears a flattop cap with a sprig of honeysuckle fixed to it, and a home-cut poacher's outfit of brown corduroy. She carries a soiled, rumpled sack under her arm. She looks jaunty, but thin necked, seedy. "What are you doing here?" she demands brusquely. "What am I doing here?" I repeat, taken aback by her bluntness and her whole appearance. "I'm—I'm looking—for some things," I stammer. "Looking for what things?" she presses. "I don't know—things—credit cards," I reply awkwardly. "Maybe part of a car." She scowls derisively. "A *car*? What would a car be doing here?" she snorts. I gesture in confusion. "I don't know—I'm *dreaming*!" I protest. "For God's sake, this is my dream," I cry. "How dare you grill me about what I can or cannot look for in it!" Just like that we're back on the same weird, antagonistic footing. "Well don't look around here again, look somewhere else," she says. "What a thing to say . . ." I exclaim, pained and piqued. "Don't worry, this is a complete accident, you won't ever see me again, I can assure you!"

There's a forlorn, hollow silence. My heart twangs, like a cold instrument fashioned out of bruises. The fragrant forest air feels stunned and disjointed, gone numb. "I'm so sorry, about everything, about what I did," I blurt out in a hushed voice. She shrugs. She doesn't say anything. "You haven't cut it off," I go on softly. "It won't come off," she retorts with bitter emphasis. She glares at me. She stares away into the rhododendrons. There's another silence. She looks lovely, but so strange, so disorienting, truly grotesque and gone-wild, like a being from an inaccessible arboreal culture. A terrible guilt laps me. "I'm really so sorry," I whisper again, feeling my legs tremble. She turns her luxuriantly modified head slowly toward me, and I get a glimpse, for just a moment, of her pain's profound fierceness. "You shouldn't have tried to take photographs," she says quietly, fixing her gaze on me from under the honeysuckled bill of her cap. "It's one thing to revenge yourself in private between the two of us—but to try to humiliate me publicly, in my professional life—" Her voice rises. I stare with hot cheeks at the ground. "I know," I murmur. "You just made me so angry." She harumphs. "And I can just imagine, you've been writing all about us—about this," she adds witheringly. "No, no—of course not," I assure her, in a harried, lame voice. "Well, maybe a bit," I confess. "But only with affection, with great respect!" "Well it better be like that," she says. "It is," I promise, growing wretched all at once. "Really, it is. . . ." There's silence again. I feel miserable. I wish the encounter would end, I realize; but the prospect swells with sorrow. "So what do you have there in that sack, a rabbit for dinner?" I murmur forlornly. "Never mind," she retorts. She twists her grip tighter. Her look turns defiant again. "It's really simply none of your business!" she informs me, agitated. The latent premises of this statement are too conceptually provoking, besides their hostility, for me to restrain myself. "Listen, I don't mean to start an argument, but how can you pronounce such incredible *notions*?" I protest, my adrenaline heating in the old way. "I mean, don't you understand, this is *my dream,* for Christ's sake, you're a figment of *my never-sleeping imagination*!" "So what? That doesn't mean you *own* me!" she cries back. A wild, astounding distraction inhabits her eyes. It robs me of speech. "Now I'm going," she cries, "and don't you dare follow me!"

She hefts the sack under her arm and turns on her heel and sets off tramping through the underbrush. The golden loads of her mustache flap out over either side of her corduroy collar, seen from behind. This is the final image I receive of her, from which I turn away after a few moments, long before she has disappeared into the greenery. I just turn away, with a broken-off, half-aired groan of exasperation, and walk in the opposite direction from her.

And she's gone from my world, from then on, and forever.

11.

At the Clockmaker's

At the Clockmaker's

After the procedure, I convalesce in a little corner room of planked walls crowded under the eaves. It's not exactly commodious, but fresh air and warmth enter through the bright, parted curtains of the window, and at day's end, the clockmaker's wife comes to wheel me out onto the porch. I sit with the tartan blanket over my lap, in the company of the other customer here. The lake shines below us through the creaking poles of the pine trees, and the ducks slowly lift their kite-tail colonies into the air and start their beat across our panorama. The air smells of resin in a softly bracing way.

My companion-in-repair and I exchange our customary daily inquiries and reports. We're casualties of romance, the two of us, and of a very particular breed: our hearts, it turns out, are cuckoo clocks. That's the kind of guys we are, and we've come here into the pine woods to have things mended. In my case, the clockmaker has had to completely remove the antique, hand-carved resident robin, so badly mangled was it in the disaster of a love affair. Its replacement alas resembles more a chickadee, and it doesn't pop from its walnut-wood hatch with quite the zing of the former much-beloved model. I'm staying on these several days more while the clockmaker continues to tinker, as he does with my colleague, whose splendid minideer antlers snapped in several places when he caught his wife cheating, for the third time. Then his spring mechanism succumbed to inner rust, and his minute hand simply stopped.

So we sit together taking the air, and the clockmaker appears with his clay pipe unlit in his teeth and his green box of tools. He bids good evening. "Whose turn first tonight?" he inquires. It's mine, and I tell him how my day went. He listens, nodding. With a finger he steadies the little acorn-weighted pendulum in front of my chest, and probes, and sets to work with his tiny file and diminutive screwdriver. I smell his warm, tobacco- and coffee-scented breath as he feels in with the thin tube of the oilcan. The oil is cool as it drips and I give a ticklish laugh. The clockmaker grins, absorbed, and shifts his pipe and coaxes the wooden tenant out between fingertips. He maneuvers it back and forth a few times, to work the oil into the mechanism. "That should be better now," he says finally. He consults his pocket watch and resets my time.

Then he turns his attention to his other charge, and I look on, marveling again at his delicacy and dexterity, so unexpected from the bluntness and haleness of his appearance. He reminds me of an oak stump in a field.

He finishes his adjustments to my neighbor, and steps back, wiping his fingers on his venerable suede apron. "Alright, gentlemen," he declares, and he looks from one to the other of us, like a conductor readying his band. There's a pause, then the hour strikes in each of our convalescing chests, and on cue the dainty shutters spring open and our birdies thrust their way proudly into public—my rotund chickadee, my colleague's funny little hen (a design notion courtesy of his mother . . .). Zestfully they deliver their exclamations. The clockmaker bends his head to attend each in turn, listening for fluency and nimbleness, for soundness of chime. When the shutters have closed, he wags a thoughtful finger in my direction. "Not quite true yet," he says. "But it's a change of wood, which always makes for a difficult balance." "It's just not the old design, is it?" I muse, on a wistful note. "But it's a very fine one; and it'll last you for years," he says, reassuring me.

He leaves us, and we sit before the darkening view until it's time for supper back in our rooms. We're still not quite strong enough for the common table, so our own society will have to stand us for the evening. We chat, as ever, about what others on this porch have always talked about—what calamities brought us hither, what prospects might await, once repairs here are complete. And of course, the abiding, quaintly embarrassing, mystery of it all, of being men whose hearts are kitschy gadgets, whose loving souls consist of petite decorated wooden cabinets—knickknack places excerpted from children's books, and occupied by handcrafted simulacra of diminutive, domesticated wildlife. Whose song is the eternal, merry outcry of the goofball and the lunatic: two syllables! two syllables! My companion sighs and gestures to himself, and exclaims disconsolately, as he does at some point every evening, "Ah, it's so hard to find a woman, who really understands . . . all this!" I have to nod in agreement, sitting beside him, feeling the slow, regular weight of my pendulum.

Around us the evening shadows knit into the fabric of one continuous darkness. Early stars hang like ornaments among the top black branches of the pines. The cry of a lone, separated bird drifts from the lake; and the clockmaker's wife comes out onto the porch with her lantern.